GULLY WASHER

FAIRY TALES OF A TRAILER PARK QUEEN
BOOK FIVE

GULLY WASHER

FAIRY TALES OF A TRAILER PARK QUEEN, BOOK 5

KIMBRA SWAIN

CRIMSON SUN
PRESS

Kimbra Swain
Gully Washer, Fairy Tales of a Trailer Park Queen, Book 5
©2018, Kimbra Swain / Crimson Sun Press, LLC
kimbraswain@gmail.com

Book Cover by: Audrey Logsdon
Formatting by Serendipity Formats: https://serendipityformats.wixsite.com/formats
Editing by Carol Tietsworth: https://www.facebook.com/Editing-by-Carol-Tietsworth-328303247526664/

CRIMSON SUN

PRESS

A NOTE FROM THE AUTHOR

When I first started writing Gully Washer, I knew that it would be a long book if I covered all the bases that I wanted to with regards to the story. It's a big story to tell, so the story arc in Gully Washer is continued in Moonshine in a Mason Jar and finished in Hotter Than Blue Blazes. Generally, I try to wrap up a story and just carry over the main arc. But with these three books, the story carries over.

On my website, you will find a list of the Fairy Tales of a Trailer Park Queen book titles. There will be 15 books and a few short stories. I know the series is lengthy, but I promise to make them all fantastic reads for those of you who love these books.

Thank you so much for your continued support and outpouring of love.

-Kimbra

CHAPTER ONE

THE STREAM RUSHED LAZILY OVER THE STONES CREATING A CALMING gurgle as Dylan and I sat on a blanket under the canopy of trees. He had packed a picnic lunch for us since it was his day off from the sheriff's department. It was official. He was the Sheriff of Lowden County again. Thankfully, today he wore torn jeans and a blue t-shirt with a Pepsi logo on the front, instead of the tans and browns of his uniform. We snacked on cheese, crackers, and wine.

"Beautiful," he said, taking in the scenery.

"Dylan, if you are about to drop a lame come-on line, let me attest, I'm a sure thing," I said.

"It's a nice day. Why must you ruin it?" he asked, laughing at me anyway.

I winked at him. "I'm sorry. What were you saying?"

"You are beautiful," he continued.

"Why thank you, Sheriff Riggs. You want to wade out into the water with me?" I asked.

"No, I'd rather take you home and bed you," he said.

"You remember the last time we were here?" I asked.

"I do," he said. "You stood out there in the water, splashing me.

You had on a white skirt tied up at your hip. I kept hoping you would bust your ass so it would get wet and I could see through it."

"Well, I never," I scoffed.

"You never what?" he asked, rolling up on his elbows to look at me.

"Very crude, Sheriff," I replied.

He shrugged, "I come by it honestly. Now, why don't you go wade on out there and fall down for me," he said. "I'll rescue you."

I laughed, and it echoed through the trees. On my knees, I crossed over to where he was lounging. Planting myself between the food and his warm body, I said, "There is no one out here. How about a little outdoor fun?" I ran my hand up under his shirt. He laid back on his back, groaning as I raked my fingernails down his chest.

Then, we realized that we weren't as alone as we thought.

"Hey Grace!" a voice called out from the water.

Dylan raised up to look at Cletus and Tater on some kind of contraption in the creek.

"What the hell?" Dylan muttered.

They each balanced on their own raft made entirely of plastic two-liter bottles. They held poles to push themselves along made of PVC pipe.

"I thought y'all gave up on that foolish boat idea," I said to them. After the tornado in the trailer park, their supply of plastic bottles had been scattered across half the county. We had to have a clean-up day just to try to minimize the damage.

"Well, we did. It was a bit ambitious," Cletus said.

"Yeah, so we made rafts," Tater added.

"It's Huck Finn and Tom Sawyer," I said.

"No, Grace, it's me, Cletus. I don't look like my cousin Tom," he said.

"Your last name is Sawyer?" I asked.

"Yeah, 'tis," he replied.

"Mine is too," Tater added.

"Y'all are kin?" I asked.

"Naw. But we have the same last name. Cletus and Tater Sawyer," Cletus explained.

"You have to be related," Dylan said.

"Nah, but he's like a brother to me, so we might as well be," Cletus said.

I sat with my mouth open, astonished at the absurdity of it. Looking at Dylan, he smirked, because I was so dumbfounded. I shook my head in disbelief.

"You guys have fun, but don't make me send out a search party because you got lost on your bottle rafts," Dylan said.

"We made one for you too, Sheriff," Tater said. "It's back at the trailer."

"That's mighty kind of you," Dylan said.

"Grace, you can go back to seducing Dylan now," Cletus said. Dylan coughed uncomfortably.

"Move along, boys," I called out to them. They pushed off down the creek, and I looked back at Dylan. "Those two crack me up."

"I had no idea what their last name was either," Dylan said. "But, I'm sure there was some talk about seducing." Dylan grabbed my wrist, pulling my body back to his.

"Cletus said something about it. Want me to call him back?" I asked.

"No. Come here," he said, rolling me over on top of him. My brown hair cascaded down around our faces. He pushed it back, grinning up at me. "Like I said, beautiful."

"The blue eyes don't bother you?" I asked because I had never been successful at restoring my brown-eyed glamour for any long period. At least, my hair was brown.

"No, Grace. I love every part of you. The fake parts as well as the real parts," he said.

I laid down with my head on his chest. Taking deep breaths, I tried to calm my inner self. It had almost been a full cycle since the last full moon, and I wasn't pregnant. I was convinced that there was something wrong with me. I'd consulted several seers and mystics, but all of them assured me that I wasn't barren. Physically, I could produce a child. I just hadn't yet.

"Talk to me," he urged.

"I'm not pregnant," I said.

"I know that," he said.

"I feel like I'm failing you," I muttered. He rolled me over on my back, hovering above me.

"Grace, if we never have a child together, I will love you until the day that I draw my last breath. If I don't have an heir, so be it. I wouldn't want to be anywhere or with anyone except with you," he said.

A tear trickled down my cheek because it was almost sweet. Okay. It was sweet. Way too sweet. Sappy, lovey-dovey sweet. Damn. I loved this man. Every single part of him. I wanted to give him a child so badly. I had even asked my father's ghost about it. He assured me that it would happen when the fates deemed it to be. The fates needed to hurry the fuck up.

"Besides if it weren't for you, I wouldn't have Winnie. I get to have a little girl which is more than I ever expected," he said.

"What do you mean?" I asked.

"If you get pregnant, it will be a boy. The Phoenix heir is always male. One Phoenix. One heir," he said.

"You can only produce male offspring?" I asked.

"Only male, and only one," he said.

"You can't have more than one child?!" I exclaimed.

"Just one," he said. "So, if that means that I get a regular gravy swappin' date with my beautiful Grace every full moon until it happens, then sign me up. I'm all for that!" He smiled, quite satisfied with himself. And me, I supposed.

"You know we do it more often than that," I said.

"Like right now?" he asked, as he shifted his hips between my legs.

I whimpered, "What about public indecency, Officer?"

"Screw the law," he said.

"I'd rather you screw me," I said.

"I'm gonna do that too," he laughed.

"Then you will wade in the water with me," I said.

"Then I will do whatever you want," he muttered as he peppered kisses down my neck.

I made sure to tuck that one away for later use. He did say *whatever* I wanted.

CHAPTER TWO

Vaguely I remember Dylan kissing me goodbye before he left for work. I awoke the second time to someone banging with a hammer outside. I threw on a robe and rushed out the front door.

"What on the mother's green earth is going on out here?" I yelled.

Levi, already pouring sweat, looked up at me with two nails in his mouth, a hammer in his hand and an unrighteous grin on his face. "Morning, Grace. Nice robe," he said.

"Dublin, what are you doing?" I said looking around at the pile of wood outside the trailer.

"Building you a porch," he said.

"But..." I started.

"You said you wanted a porch. I'm building you a porch," he explained. He already had posts placed and had poured concrete around them. He was working on a frame.

"Where did you learn to build porches?" I asked.

"Texas," he drawled.

"Did you learn to do everything in Texas?" I asked.

He looked up at me with a grin. "There are a few things I learned in Alabama," he said.

"Like what?"

"I'll tell ya later. When I know Dylan won't kill me," he said.

I rolled my eyes. I was pretty sure I knew every trick in his book and then some. He didn't impress me. In fact, I'd been meaning to have a talk with my bard. I'd heard reports through town that he was on quite the bender. A Sexual bender.

It wasn't so long ago I warned Ella Jenkins to calm herself during a binge, and here was my own bard fucking every female in town. It wouldn't be long, and he would be out of candidates. I felt responsible. I knew why he was doing it, and it made it that much tougher to tell him to stop. I could order him to stop. He was still my servant, but he also held a piece of my heart which I hated.

"Why don't you go fix me something cold to drink?" he said.

"Damn, Dublin. I ain't your maid," I said, stomping back into the trailer.

Winnie was spending the night with Nestor and Mable, so I didn't have to worry about getting her ready for school. I looked at the clock on the stove. It was almost noon. I picked up my cell phone where I found several messages from Dylan. Most of them were just sweet, but the last one caught my attention.

Dylan: Finely is coming by after lunch. He says it's ready.

I responded to that one.

Me: The vault?
Dylan: *wink*

"Woot!" I exclaimed as Rufus ran around my feet. I snuggled him for a minute then poured him some dog food. Jumping in the shower, I realized that I never brought Levi a glass of water. Oops!

When I walked into my bedroom naked as a jaybird, I looked to see him standing with his shirt off in the living room bent over in front of the window air conditioner unit.

"Fuck!" I said, rushing to the door. I slammed it before he could turn around.

"I saw enough," he teased.

"Shut up, Levi," I yelled at him through the door.

"Where you going?" he asked.

"Finley is coming," I said.

"Oh, yeah. Seems I remember him telling me about something today," he said as he dug through the refrigerator.

I slipped into a pair of shorts and a t-shirt. When I went into the kitchen, Levi leaned on the counter drinking a cold soda. He watched me take an orange one out of the fridge. I popped the top and turned to him. His eyes were on my ass.

"Levi! You and I are going to have a talk," I said.

"I know what you are going to say, and I don't care," he said.

"You've got to stop this," I said.

"Why? I'm not forcing anyone to sleep with me. I'm just having a good time. Sowing my wild oats," he said.

"Your wild oats are going to sprout stalks all over this town," I said.

"Nah. I always pull out," he said. My jaw dropped open. He laughed at me. "Come on, Grace. You aren't a prude."

I sat down in my recliner on the edge. Taking a deep breath, I looked at him. His face changed from cocky manwhore to my sweet bard. "Levi, please just calm it down a little. I'm afraid you are going to get entangled with the wrong fairy."

He put his hands on his hips, and a growl escaped his lips. "I've already done that!" he shouted. At first, I thought he meant Riley, but it was clear he meant me. Our connection wasn't as strong as it used to be after he moved out of the trailer, but in moments like that, I had no doubt of what he meant.

"Right," I said, standing up to go let Rufus out.

"Grace," Levi said trying to get my attention. He regretted it, but the damage was done.

"Your wild oats are waiting, Levi," I replied heading into the front yard with Rufus.

Levi rushed out the door behind me. Instead of talking to me, he spoke to our newest neighbor, Jenny. "Oh, hello Jenny." Jenny stood at the end of the drive. No doubt she had heard us arguing in the trailer. The walls were paper thin. I had reinforced them with a spell after the sylph incident, but I needed to soundproof them.

"Hey, Levi. I've come to talk to Grace," she said. Jenny moved into the park in the next to the last spot we had available. Shortly after, another trailer moved in, but we had never seen the occupant. I didn't mind people who kept to themselves. I was once the same way.

"What's going on?" I asked.

"Walk with me down to my trailer," she said with a smile. Jenny was a grindylow. She had seen our fight with the sylph. She had also seen my royal crown. After talking to her, I decided that I liked her. Grindies were generally mean. Scary even. In fact, there were rumors that Jenny had green teeth, but contrary to that belief, her teeth were white, except the front two which were 24 karat gold caps.

I walked with her down to the trailer. "How's Levi?" she asked.

"Bingeing," I replied.

"That sucks. He will grow out of it," she said.

"I never did," I replied. She laughed.

"Neither did I, but I promise not to touch your bard," she said.

"I can't keep him from doing what he wants to do," I replied.

"Of course, you can. You are the queen."

"True, but I hate ordering him. Somehow, I think this is something he needs to learn on his own," I said as we approached the end of the drive. Looking past her trailer I could see that there was standing water in the forest beyond the trailer. "The swamp coming to you?"

"I didn't summon it if that's what you are implying," she said defensively.

I waved her off. "Wonder if that's left from all that rain we got," I replied.

"Perhaps, but occasionally it smells," she said crinkling her nose. She had a spattering of brown freckles across it. She actually looked rather plain for a fairy girl, but cute in her own way. She didn't wear a glamour, but she did have an animal shift. I'd never seen one, but I heard that it was like a cross between an octopus and an iguana. I took a deep breath. It smelled like rot. I turned to the quiet trailer across from hers.

"Smell is coming from that," I said. I looked over the trailer in question. It was surrounded by a green glowing ward. Summer fairy.

"Summer," she said.

"You can see the ward?" I asked.

"Yep. It's a mean one too," she said.

"Yes, it is," I replied, as Levi joined us.

"Grace, Finley is here," he said.

"Thanks, Levi. I'll check on the water, Jenny. Perhaps, folks that have lived here longer than I might know why it's gathering behind the park," I said.

"Thanks, Grace. Tell Finley I said hello. I may not touch your bard, but I'll be happy to entertain that fair-skinned brother of yours," she smiled.

"He's usually open to anything," I grumbled. Trudging back up the hill, Levi reached out and touched my tattoo. I stopped instinctively.

His voice erupted through my head. "*I didn't mean it,*" he said.

"*Sure, you did,*" I replied. "*I know what you think of me now.*" A sex binge could make you arrogant, cocky and mouthy, but most of the time it was the truth. Levi currently had no filter. He meant it. He just regretted that he meant it. I still loved him, but I hated this stage he was in. More than anything, I missed my best friend, but everything had changed now. I supposed those days were gone.

"*No, Grace. I didn't mean it. I swear it. Even now, all I want is you,*" he said.

I jerked my arm away from him. His eyes darkened. "I'll finish the deck later," he said blinking out of sight.

CHAPTER THREE

Finley stood next to one of the posts Levi had laid for the new porch. He looked at his cell phone grinning. He was addicted to the damn thing. He decided against a glamour since most everyone in town was supernaturally inclined or knew enough about us not to care. His white hair hung to his waist, but he had it pulled back and tied behind his head. A week ago, he walked around town with a man bun. Levi teased him calling it a twat knot. Dylan emphasized it by saying that when he sees bun he thinks that there is a serious blow job in his future. I scowled at that notion, but Finley stopped wearing it the next day. Finley said he saw it on the internet that it was the hip thing to do, and that he was trying to fit in. Dylan gave him a Coors ball cap. To be honest, he looked better in the man bun as opposed to the hat with the tips of his ears pointed up beside it.

"Why aren't your ears pointed?" Levi asked me at the time.

"I got them clipped," I replied. He took it for the truth, and I never explained otherwise. I supposed that when I dropped my glamour he never noticed the subtle tips to my ears under all that hair.

Finley and I had a talk about not believing everything he read on the internet. He was starting to figure it all out, but in the meantime, it was extremely amusing.

"Morning, Glory," he called out to me as I walked up.

"Hey Fin, what's up?"

"Where did Levi go?" he asked.

"He got his panties in a wad, and I'm sure he's brooding somewhere," I said.

"Or fucking something," Finley added. He noticed the sour look on my face and muttered an apology.

I took a deep breath. "That's why he's mad. I tried to convince him that the binge had gone on long enough. He lashed out at me," I said.

"He will figure it all out, Sis. Give him time. Besides the binge isn't as bad as you think," he said. "Come on. Let's go down to the Food Mart."

"You came to visit so I could take you to the grocery store?" I asked.

"Sort of," he grinned like the devil.

"You are up to no good," I said. "I thought the vault was finished."

He tucked the phone into his pocket without another word then climbed into my truck. His aqua eyes glittered with excitement as he waved me to the truck. I grabbed my keys from inside, and we drove to town, which took all of two minutes.

As I pulled into the parking lot, I stopped in the middle of the street. Henrietta Purcell was behind me in her Pepto pink bug and almost rammed me. I could not believe my eyes. I suppose Henrietta couldn't see the spectacle beyond my big red truck.

"What is that?" I asked.

Finley grinned, "Isn't it great?"

"I've never seen anything like it," I replied.

Henrietta honked her horn. I pulled further into the lot and then to the side because I needed to process what I was seeing. At the end of the strip mall that held the tattoo shop, the Food Mart, and a couple of other small businesses, a single wide trailer sat with a funkadelic sign that said, "Magic Vape." A mural was painted on the whole side of the trailer which was a giant rainbow with white, puffy clouds. Next to a unicorn with a crystalline horn, a bold font proclaimed, "Without clouds, there can be no rainbows."

I parked the truck on the far side of the lot. Stepping out to view the shop, I asked Finley, "Is that glitter paint?" The whole thing reflected light in a spectrum of colors.

Finley laughed, "It's awesome! Let's go check it out."

"I don't want to go to a magical vape shop," I said.

"It is April 20th. I was told you are supposed to smoke on this day," Finley said.

I rolled my eyes. His lack of knowledge of the real world frightened and amused me. "They are talking about marijuana."

"Oh. Well, maybe they have some," he suggested.

"Vape is like a mechanical smoking pipe," I said. "It's not real smoke. Chris Purcell may never step foot in town again after this."

"Oh," he said. "I still want to see. It's fucking glitter rainbows!" He pointed at it like an excited child. I had to admit I was curious.

"Okay," I relented. He practically skipped across the parking lot in happy glee. There was no practical about it. He skipped. "Slow down, Edward."

"Who is Edward?" he asked.

"Sparkly vamp," I replied.

"I'm not a vamp! I just happen to like to bite my women," he grinned.

"T. M. I. You are my brother. I don't want to hear that shit," I said.

He laughed as he stepped up on the wooden steps that led to the glitter-covered door. He opened it for me, and we stepped inside. Smoke wafted around the room and billowed out of the open door. There were no walls in the trailer, but the shelves were lined with various liquids and vape mods.

"Good afternoon, Grace, Queen of the Exiles," a tattooed man behind the counter said. He leaned on the counter taking puffs off his mod. When I say tattooed, I mean every part of his body, including the top of his head was inked. "Nice tat." He nodded to my arm.

"Um, thanks," I replied rubbing my arm instinctively. I rarely had to charge my tattoo anymore. After pulling my father's power in the confrontation with the sylph, I held on to it. The longer I kept it, the easier it was to control. The exhaustion from before wasn't as bad. Dylan suspected that it wore me out because I fought it. He told me to give into the power. While it sounded easy to do, I was still apprehensive about letting it control me.

"Smells good," Finley said. The room smelled like glazed doughnuts. It was heavenly. Perhaps I needed a vape just to smell it. Of course, I could just light a candle, too.

"How can I help you, my Queen?" the man asked.

"What's your name?" I returned the question.

"Míchean Artair. Most folks call me Mike," he said, offering me his hand.

I shook it lightly, but the ripple of a very powerful magic wielder ran up my arm. I hadn't even thought to see what kind of fairy he was. He grinned watching me figure it out. As I looked at him, I realized he wasn't exactly a fairy at all, but had the ability to use fairy magic. There were only a few of his kind left on earth that I knew of. Once I saw his clothing I pieced it all together. He wore overalls covered in patches. The shirt underneath was torn and tattered. He could pass for a beggar.

"Oh, you are one of *those*," I said.

"Yes, ma'am," he replied. I supposed he knew I could tell what he was.

"What do you think of the shop?" he asked.

"It's interesting. I had no idea that fairies used vapes," I said.

"Everyone should vape," he said.

I shook my head, "I don't think so."

"Hey, Glory, come look at this one," Finley said, picking up a bottle of the liquid.

"Whiskey flavor. That's what I'm talking about," I said.

"I figured you would like that one," he smiled.

"Do they have cunt flavor? I'm pretty sure that would be yours," I said. He punched me in the arm.

"Maybe. I'll buy a bottle of it for Levi," he teased back. He immediately realized that he'd forgotten that Levi was a sore subject and apologized, again.

"It's okay," I said, walking around the room to see what all Mike had to offer. Switching to fairy sight, I realized the room was divided into two different kinds of liquids. Some pulsed with magical powers, while the other rested in their bottles with no supernatural glow. "Magic liquids. What do they do?"

"Different things," Mike said. "I've got a potion for just about every fairy aliment."

"Do you have one to stop a sexual binge?" I asked.

Mike laughed. "Yes, it's called granny panties."

"Seriously?"

"I've got liquid for everything," Mike professed. "How about I show you my private collection?"

"Um, no thanks," I said dismissing him. He continued.

"I meant no offense. I've got a back room that you might like," he smiled.

"Kinky," I laughed, thinking he was still hitting on me.

"My Queen, you should see the secret room," he said, waving his hand over the floor in front of the desk. I felt a ward pop up on the inside of the trailer. Finley was beside me quickly. My tattoo flared with blue power.

"It's okay. Come see," Finley said, calming me. All the humor had left his voice. He took my hand, leading me down a dark staircase. When we reached the bottom, I realized we were underground. I knew that dank smell. Finley cast a small spell to illuminate the room. The walls glittered like the outside of the trailer, only these walls weren't covered in glitter. Gemstones embedded in the walls flickered with an unnatural light. Beyond us, a large door with a circle triquetra carved in the center. Surrounding the triquetra was the skull head of a stag. Its antlers encased the circle symbol. It was the same as the symbol on Finley's cloak.

"What is this?" I said looking at him.

"Your vault," he smiled.

"My vault is under a vape shop run by a Solomonar?" I asked. I wondered if Mike had his own personal dragon or if he just rode whatever one he could find. The Solomonar were pulled from the human population and taught to use magic. A wizard of sorts. They were best known as dragon riders. They had the ability to control the wind, rain, and hail. Very powerful humans who could tap into fairy magic. Once they tapped into that magic, they became immortal. Most of them hailed from Romania, but when their numbers dwindled, the Solomonar sought others to join their ranks.

"Your supernatural identification is getting better. Stop stalling. Walk toward the door," he insisted.

Pushing me forward with his hand on my back, the door began to shift and change. The circle triquetra stayed the same, but instead of the stag head, the knot was surrounded by filigree matching my tattoo.

"What? No unicorn?" I asked.

"I figured you wanted to keep that one on the down low," he said. "Did I use those words right?"

"What words?"

"Down low?" he said.

I chuckled, "Yes, you did. Congrats, you are mastering modern slang," I said. "There is no knob or handle."

"It's a portal. Just walk through," he said.

The doorway hummed with power as I approached it. Switching again to fairy sight, I saw through to the other side. I walked through into a cavern. The walls were covered in shelves with old books and artifacts. In the center of the room, there were twelve pedestals in the shape of a clock. The three, six, nine and twelve towers had a single fixture to hold a stone. The three and six spots were empty. I felt the air and fire power stones in my pocket.

"Can I leave them here?" I asked, pulling them out of my pocket to show Finley.

"Please tell me you don't just walk around with those in your pocket," he said.

"Yeah, who is going to take it from me?" I asked, raising an eyebrow.

"Good point. Yes, you can leave them here. You should be able to access them, but since the stones were given to you by their keeper you don't need them with you. As for the other two, I haven't yet located their handlers. I'm still looking," he said.

I placed the fire and air stones in their proper places. The earth stone sitting at the top of the clock was a black, slick piece of obsidian. It was domed, polished and smooth. When I got closer it seemed to shimmer with an iridescence. I knew I couldn't use it, because it hadn't been given to me, but it was a lovely, raven stone.

Finally, I turned to the water stone as Finley watched. The orb was about 1 inch in diameter, and it seemed to be filled with water which rolled and tossed around the edges like a stormy sea, but when I got closer it wasn't water at all. It was a sea of tiny sapphires and topaz that undulated like the ocean. It was mesmerizing.

"No rush," I said. "This one is spectacular."

"Yes, it is. They are each unique in their own way," he said. "All of this is your inheritance, Glory."

"Our inheritance," I corrected him.

"You are the leader here," he said.

"In truth, you can't have a leader without the right support, so in that, it belongs to all of us here in Shady Grove. At least those that follow me. The rest can take a long walk off a short pier," I said.

He laughed. "You are crazy."

"Proud of it, too," I added. "I have no use for any of this."

"You will. Just try to remember what all is here. If there are things you know of that exist, I can track them down for you too," he said.

Before I turned to leave, in the back, an empty book pedestal stood. I locked eyes on it. "I want that book back," I said.

"I'm not sure why you let them have it at all," Finley said. "Have you heard from Jeremiah?"

"No. The last I heard was that he and Riley are in Rhiannon's realm, preparing for war with Brock," I said.

"Do you think we should help them?" Finley asked.

"Do you think Rhiannon would accept our help?" I replied.

"Probably not," he said.

"Then why bother? However, I want to get with Levi after the party tomorrow night, and let's make plans to shut Shady Grove off from the rest of the world," I said.

"What about the humans who are still here?" he asked.

"As far as I know, Cletus, Tater, and Winnie are the only ones left," I said.

"Perhaps. We should check with Troy to be sure," he said.

"Dylan is the sheriff again," I corrected.

"That's right. Well, he would know, I suppose," he said.

"We will double check," I said. "It protects the humans as well as us until we decide what to do about the Otherworld," I said. "I've got a party to finish planning. Are you coming?"

"I wouldn't miss it," he said. "Do you think he knows?"

"I hope not. Super-secret," I replied.

I dropped Finley off at his apartment. I could feel Levi inside. He wasn't alone. There was nothing I could do about that right now unless I could convince him to vape some granny panties. Besides, I had a surprise birthday party to plan.

CHAPTER FOUR

PACING AROUND THE TRAILER, I TRIED TO THINK OF ANYTHING I'D forgotten. Hopefully, everything would be perfect for the party. Tabitha would be by to pick up Winnie who had retreated to her bedroom to play with Bramble and Briar. They were excited to see her, but even more excited to get another night of fairy boinking without her here. I was pretty sure Bramble could give Levi a run for his money in the gravy-swapping business.

It struck me as a crazy, fun idea to throw a surprise birthday party for Dylan. He once told me he didn't have a birthday. So, I had Remington Blake do some digging for me, and he found a record of when Dylan was born. I just hated that Remy found the record a week ago, and I only had a week to plan. It would be a double whammy. "Surprise, it's your birthday that you didn't know you were having," I muttered to myself. Rufus raised his head to see if I was talking to him. I scratched him along his back and he grunted.

To add to all of it, it was finally a full moon again. The party would be after dark at the bar. Nestor and Mable were setting it up for me because I wanted to be home when he got here. I suppose he wouldn't be suspicious since he didn't even realize how important today was to those of us who cared about him.

"Grace," Tabitha said.

"Oh, hey! I didn't hear you come in," I said. "Winnie! Time to go!"

"She playing with the fairies?" she asked.

"Yes," I replied.

"You know she's probably the only human left at the school," she said.

"She is. I'm just glad she doesn't realize that," I said.

"Has she talked to you about her best friend?" Tabitha asked.

"No, who is it?" I asked.

"Mark Capps," she said.

"What? The wolf boy. Oh, hell no! No daughter of mine is going to hang out with a wolf!" I protested. Tabitha looked at me with her eyebrows raised.

"What was that you said at the council meeting? It's time to get over petty prejudices," she laughed.

"I was talking about a were-hog living in a fairy neighborhood! Not a wolf playing with my daughter!" I said.

"What wolf?" Dylan said as he entered the door.

"Your daughter's best friend in school is Mark Capps!" I said, shaking my finger in the direction of Winnie's room.

His panty-melting grin crossed his face. "Damn it, woman! I love you," he laughed.

I stuck my bottom lip out. "Aren't you concerned?" I asked.

He sauntered over ignoring Tabitha, cupped my face and said, "No. I'm not. He's a good kid." Then he kissed me.

"That's not fair," I pouted.

"Hey, Tabitha," he said without looking at her.

"I'll just get Winnie," she said.

As she walked into Winnie's room, I heard the two fairies helping Winnie get all of her overnight things. She walked out with Tab while Dylan stayed focused on me.

"Daddy!" That's all it took, and his attention was torn away from smoldering me to death.

"Pumpkin! How are you?" he asked lifting her up above his head.

"I'm so excited to go with my friend, Tabitha. We are going to get ice cream," she said.

"Awesome. Just don't eat all of mine," he said.

"I couldn't eat that much, silly Daddy," she said, laughing at him. I think his interaction with her turned me on more than the smolder.

"If you don't save me some, I'll have to eat your belly," he said as he made chomping noises on her stomach. She squealed with delight until he let her go. "I love you, Winnie. Be good."

"Yes, sir. Bye, Momma," she said waving at me.

As Tabitha and Winnie got in the car, Dylan waved his hand toward the door. A wave of heat crossed the room slamming it shut. He blinked to fire consuming his clothes, then back to human, in an instant. The next thing I knew, I was backed against the bedroom door with my azure flaming- eyed fiancé pressed against me.

"Whoa! Slow down there, Dylan," I said.

"I hope you didn't have plans tonight, because I am going to keep you naked in bed all night," he smiled.

"Actually, I promised Nestor we would drop by the bar later," I said, hoping that he wouldn't protest.

He pulled my shirt off over my head. His warm hands worked down to my hips to unzip my jeans. Planting kisses between my breasts, he made a line to my neck with his tongue. I found it hard to focus on the task at hand which was convincing him to go to Hot Tin later.

"You are distracted," he groaned in my ear.

"I'm with you. I just need to keep my promise, too," I said.

"When?"

"A couple of hours," I replied.

He sighed. "I suppose we could take a drink break, but we don't have time to goof off." He sounded all authoritative. It was cute.

"Sure thing, Sheriff. Why don't you cuff me to make sure I don't goof off?" I said.

He flamed across the room where he laid his jacket, and back again. Suddenly my hands were cuffed together.

"There," he said.

"You keep flaming across this room, and this whole thing will go up like a tinderbox," I scolded.

"You are going to have to hush your mouth. Don't make me do it for you," he grinned.

"Holy shit! What has gotten into you?" I asked.

"We are doing it this time. Making a baby," he said, as he grabbed my cuffed wrists. He dragged me to the bed, then produced a second set of cuffs to attach me to the headboard. Now I knew why he wanted the wrought iron bed instead of the wooden one. Kinky bastard.

"I'm not sure I like this," I said.

"Why?" he asked.

"I can't touch you," I said, hoping to gain some sympathy. It did make me feel trapped. I'd run my entire life to keep from being trapped, and here I was letting him cuff me to a bed. I pulled on the cuffs and even felt them with my power to see if I could unlatch them. I couldn't.

"There will be plenty of touching," he assured me. "But if you are worried, you can have a safe word, Queen of the Exiles. Don't give me some crap that you can't get out of those."

"I can't," I said.

"You can, too," he said.

"Where did you get these cuffs?" I asked.

"Troy," he replied.

"Hmm. Wonder if he cuffs Amanda to the bed. It would take magical cuffs to hold her down, I think," I replied. However, his tongue distracted me until the moment I realized I was actually stuck.

"Heh. You are trapped!" he laughed as he hovered over me.

"Do I get my safe word?" I asked.

"Sure. It's pickle," he said.

"No. I'm not saying that," I said.

"That's the point. I don't want you to say it," he laughed.

"This is ridiculous!" I complained, but then that distracting tongue of his found a nice spot. For the rest of the evening, the only words I spoke involved his name, a vulgar four-letter word, and yes.

~

"WHY DO we have to go to the bar tonight?" he asked as he slipped on a tight pair of jeans.

When he reached for a t-shirt, I wrinkled my nose at him. "Not that," I said, as I looked through the closet. I picked out a black button-up shirt.

"Awful fancy for Hot Tin," he said.

"Is it a crime for me to want my fiancé to look nice?" I asked.

"What are you up to?" he asked suddenly. Damn lawman.

"Nothing," I said.

"Grace, honey, I know when you are lying," he said.

"So, what if I am? I'm not telling you," I said. To change the subject, I asked, "How do I look?"

"Like I need to skip Hot Tin, and cuff you back to the bed. You look gorgeous. I'd fuck you," he said. As if he hadn't done it already a hundred times.

"High praise from the man who just had his way with me," I said. "I was defenseless."

"You were in a pickle," he said.

I stopped moving, except for shaking my head. "No, don't say that again," I said.

"It's funny. Go ahead and laugh," he said as he threatened to tickle me.

"Time to go," I proclaimed.

We drove together to Hot Tin in the truck. I was on an adrenaline high and had to suppress my fairy side. I couldn't wait until we walked in the bar. I expected every one of our friends to be there, except Tabitha who had Winnie. I dreaded seeing Levi. I just hoped I didn't have to watch him fawn all over a woman all night.

As we approached the door, Dylan slipped his hand into mine. "Thank you, Grace," he said.

25

"For what?"

"Tonight," he said.

"What? That back at the trailer? We do that all the time," I said.

"It's never the same though. I'll never get tired of making love to you," he smiled. "Let's go have a couple of drinks, then go back home. I'm not done."

"Good. Because I'm not done either," I returned his smile.

He opened the door for me, but the room was dark.

"What's going on?" he muttered, pulling me toward him to protect me.

The lights flicked on and the whole town yelled, "Surprise!"

"Huh?"

"It's your birthday," I said.

"I don't have a birthday," he muttered.

Remington Blake crossed the room and handed me a folder. "Thanks, Remy. Yes, you do. This is a signed form by Washington Blackarrow, the current chief of the Algonquin tribe. His oral records speak of a child born of fire and thunder. He places that date on April 21st. Today. Happy birthday, Darlin'."

He looked down at the papers then back at me. Troy patted him on the back which caused him to jump. "Here. You look like you need this," he said, handing him a beer.

"Grace," he said quietly. His eyes welled up. I'd never seen Dylan cry, and I didn't want him to start now.

"Hey, there. None of that," I said.

"Shit. This is amazing. I don't know how you did this," he muttered, looking from the paper to me then to Remy. A young woman I'd never seen cozied up next to Remy. I couldn't wait to ask him about her, but I turned my attention back to Dylan.

"I love you," I said.

He broke out of the daze with a laugh. He scooped me up and spun me around. "I will love you forever," he blurted out. Half the room laughed. "Oh, hey, y'all. Thanks for coming to my," he paused, running his hand through his hair nervously, "Well, to my birthday party."

There were cheers and claps. Mable entered carrying a big cake with a sheriff star on it. "Congrats on being sheriff again, and happy birthday," she said. Nestor stood behind her after she set the cake down on the bar. There were a lot of candles. I wasn't sure how many there were, but Dylan blew them out without effort. The music cranked up, and we partied.

CHAPTER FIVE

D YLAN AND T ROY WERE HAVING A HEATED GAME OF POOL WHEN L EVI
asked me to dance.

"I don't want to dance with you, Levi," I said, watching Dylan
and Troy goof off trying to make stupid shots.

"I asked him for permission," Levi said.

"Good for you. The answer is the same," I said.

He leaned into my ear, as I pulled away to look him in the eye.
"Dance with me." The command rolled over my skin, and I
groaned at the power of it. Dylan suddenly looked up at me, then at
Levi. I shook my head. Levi offered his hand to me, and I took it.
Dylan continued to joke with Troy but kept one eye on Levi.

"If you ever do that again," I started to say.

"Shut up, Grace," Levi said, playing with his power. "You
wanted me to use it more. I'm using it."

"Not on me," I said. "Is that what you are doing to these
women?"

He held me by the waist with one hand. The other rested at my
neck. "You know me better than that," he said.

"Lately, I feel like I don't know you at all," I replied.

"I know, and you are right. I have been bingeing, but it doesn't matter who I'm with. None of them are you, so I'm going to stop," he said with a sad look on his face.

We danced silently for a few minutes. No one seemed to care that we were together while Dylan played pool. He cut his eyes to us occasionally. Levi had more to say, so I waited patiently for it. Pushing him wasn't going to do me any good. He pulled me a little closer.

"Pressing your luck," I said.

"I know, but I need to tell you something," he said.

"What is it, Dublin?" I asked.

"Dublin. The place I'm from, but the only place I feel at home is with you, but I couldn't live in the trailer anymore. Moving out wasn't enough," he said.

I tried to pull away from him. I knew why now he wanted me closer. He had the leverage to hold me in place. The only way I was getting away from him was with a struggle. To make a scene. He knew I didn't want that at Dylan's party. "Levi," I gritted my teeth.

"Release me," he said.

"What?" I choked on my own word.

"You said that if I ever wanted to be released, that you would do it. I think it's the only way," he said. "I've talked to Finley about it. He seems to agree. It would break the bond. I'm leaving Shady Grove."

"No," I whispered. I couldn't stop the tears. Dylan noticed them immediately.

"Grace," he said from across the room. I bit my lip and shook my head at him.

"Don't do this," I said.

Levi pressed his forehead against mine. Dylan started to rush toward us when Finley grabbed his arm.

"Let go of me," he growled, swatting at Finley.

"Release me. Please, Grace. Put me out of this misery," he begged.

Dylan collided with us. Shoving Levi away from me. "What is wrong with you?" Dylan shouted at him.

Levi's head swayed back and forth. "I can't do it anymore, man. She's got to let me go," he said.

Dylan met my eyes. His palms rested on my cheeks covering my tears. "You decide. He is your servant. Whatever you choose, I'm here. We will work it out," he said.

"Gloriana," Levi said.

My tattoo flared turning my hair platinum. Silver swirls covered my arms, chest, and legs. The power of it was growing. "Levi Rearden, royal bard, my servant," I said working up the courage to let him go. The room stood in silence as my power built. Levi trembled because he had been named by the fairy monarch. I saw fear and doubt in him. He didn't know what he wanted for sure. I doubted myself in having the power to let him go. I opened my mouth to speak when Stephanie Davis walked into the bar.

"Did I interrupt something?" she asked.

"You are banished from this town. Why are you here?" I spat at her. I was already in royal form. The sight of her drove me to see red. The council's first business when we were gathered was to banish Stephanie and Brock. She knew it too. Coming here was a death sentence.

"Before you kill me, Grace. Not that I think you would, because you are weak…," she started to say.

"On your knees," I ordered her. Dylan had moved behind me, and I felt his hand tighten on my forearm. Stephanie dropped to her knees because she had no power here. She knew it too. Behind her stood a boy about seven years old. He looked scared. He had sandy blonde hair and striking blue eyes.

"I beg you not to kill me in front of my son," she whimpered.

"What the hell?" I muttered.

"I brought him here to be with his father. Brock will kill him if he stays in the Otherworld," she cried. The boy shifted his weight, not knowing what to do. He looked at me then quickly away.

"Who is his father?" I asked, knowing the answer.

"No," Dylan whispered to me. "No, Grace, it's not possible."

Stephanie's tears dried quickly, and an evil smile crossed her face. "He's Dylan's heir, of course."

The room turned frigid. My emotions bounced around with my father's power pressing down on me. I felt the urge to strike them both down. I fought it with everything that I had. Dylan got between me and her. "You can't protect them from me," I sputtered.

"Look at me! Grace! Look at me," he said, grabbing my chin. His hand turned to ice which he quickly melted. "No! I'm telling you. This is not my child."

"You can't know that. Look at him," I muttered. I saw Levi out of the corner of my eye. He couldn't stop me from killing them because, at the moment, the only thing stopping me was Dylan. A battle he would lose. He knew it.

He shook his head. "Levi, come here," he ordered. Levi came up to us while everyone else cowered around the room. "Take her out the back. Calm her down."

"I'm not going with him. He doesn't want to be my servant anymore," I said.

"Good thing he still is, then. I won't let you do this, Grace," Dylan warned me.

"You can't stop me," I hissed.

"I can," Levi said. He pushed Dylan out of the way taking his place in front of me. "Come with me." I had no choice but to follow him. He wrapped his arm around me, pushing me toward the side door. I watched over my shoulder as Dylan turned on Stephanie.

"You better explain yourself, whore," he said. "You fucked so many people when you lived here. You can't prove that this is my son."

"But it is," she smiled, watching Levi take me out the back door.

When we hit the cool night air, I ran. Levi kept pace behind me. When I reached the end of the strip mall close to the tattoo shop, I leaned on the wall to catch my breath. The power faded. Levi stood away from me but watched me closely.

"It can't be," I muttered. "No wonder I couldn't get pregnant."

"Grace, come on. You know Dylan loves you. He has always loved you," he said. "He told me everything from before I came along. He's always loved you. This doesn't change that."

Levi stepped closer, testing the waters. I pushed off the wall, barreling into him. I wrapped my arms around his waist and cried into his chest. He stopped talking for a long time, just holding me. Letting me cry.

"I couldn't control the urge to kill her," I said.

"It's the law, Grace. The council decided along with you that she was banished. Without an invite, she is marked for death the moment she stepped back in Shady Grove. You had no choice," he said.

He was right. When we banished them, I didn't realize that I would be the one that enforced the law, but the royal power within me took over. I wondered if it was the same for my father. I'd seen him strike down many wayward fairies. He must have had no choice in the matter once the council decided. Which meant that when the council banished me, he had no choice but to obey.

"Damn it, Levi. If you hadn't been there," I said. "If I had released you, I might have killed Dylan's son."

"I know. Now we know that I can't be free," he said. I stepped back from him.

"I'm sorry," I said. "I know you are unhappy."

"It's okay. A long time ago when Jeremiah told me I was coming here to learn from you he gave me a choice. He would dump me far away, and I could hope that the demon wouldn't find me. Or I could come here. I choose to be here. I choose to stay here. I choose to love you. I just have to live with the consequences instead of running," he said.

"You are a better person than I am. I spent my whole life running. Now look at me," I said.

He brushed his thumb across my wet cheek. "I see you. You are a queen."

Damn that boy. Levi always knew the right things to say. I just wished he was saying them to someone who deserved him. I saw Dylan come out of the bar, looking for us. He ran over to where we were.

We stood in silence. Neither of us knew what to say. Levi stepped back so that he wasn't between us, but he stayed close. I felt his presence behind me leaning on the wall of the strip mall.

"I don't know what to say," Dylan said.

"Me either," I replied.

"You. Grace. It's always been you," he said.

"I know, but there is a child. Your heir," I said.

He stepped up to me with his jaw set. "I don't care what she says. That is not my child. I would know my own child."

"Whose child is he then?" I asked.

"I'm not sure, but we will find out. Grace, she even slept with Joey Blankenship. You remember Joey, right?" he said.

"Yeah," I remembered my one-night stand prior to sleeping with Dylan. He got off. I didn't. No repeat performances. Joey ended up pretty bad off after it, and I thought perhaps I did something to him, but if Stephanie slept with him too, I was sure that it fucked him in the head. "He looked like he could have been your brother."

"Yes! It could be his child. Fairy children grow fast if the fairy parent doesn't slow their process. I'm sure Stephanie let him grow. The kid is probably only a year and a half old," he said.

"You slept with her a year and a half ago?" I asked.

He bit his lip and nodded. "I did. I was in a bad place."

"So, you went to her for comfort. You told me that you hated her," I said, trying to understand.

"It was a hate fuck. In every sense of the words. I can't take it back, Grace," he said.

"I know," I replied with a whimper. "I just don't know how much of this I can take. If that child is yours, then we have been doing all of this for nothing."

"*Nothing?* Making love to you is not *nothing* to me," he said. I knew he was in pain, too. I could see it in his eyes.

"She ruined my party," I pouted. I heard Levi snicker behind me.

"I thought it was my party," Dylan said.

"Everything is about her," Levi interjected.

"Shut your mouth, Levi Rearden. You are in enough trouble as it is," I said. A smile cracked across my face.

"See. Everything is normal," Dylan said.

"It's never normal," I said.

"Abnormal is our normal," he replied.

"Fuck me," I muttered.

"Gladly," Dylan whispered in my ear as he wrapped me up in his warm arms. "Thank you, Levi. Have you rethought this whole business?"

"Yeah. It was a bad idea," he said. "I'm gonna go hit something." He muttered to himself as he walked across the empty parking lot toward the bar.

"What do we do?" I asked.

"We should go back to the party. Granted it's a little subdued now, but we should at least make an appearance before we go home," he said.

"Is she still there?" I asked.

"No. Troy and Amanda took her down to the motel. They are getting them a room and will keep them there until the council decides what to do with her," he said.

"And the child?" I asked.

"We have to find out if he's mine," he said.

"It's like Jerry Springer," I said.

"Ugh. Yeah, I suppose it is," he groaned.

"I love that show," I replied. "I kinda hate it right now though. First the kitsune, now this. I don't know how many more episodes I can take."

He laughed at me. "Come on."

We went back to the bar, but it wasn't fun and games anymore. Nestor hugged me the moment I stepped in the door, and I almost lost my composure again. "It's going to be okay," he said.

I tried to believe him, but I didn't feel that way. Dylan and I joined Finley at a table. Betty and Luther sat nearby on stools at the bar. Nestor sat down with us along with Mable. He gave each of us a cup of coffee. Everyone else had left, including Levi. Twisting in my chair, I couldn't get comfortable. My emotions stirred inside of me.

"Drink," Nestor said.

I took a sip. It was some of his most powerful coffee. It washed over me like a spring rainstorm. My whole body calmed including my mind. I saw the fear in Dylan's eyes. I loved him. Love meant sticking with things even when it got tough. I didn't think it could get tougher than this.

"What do we do?" Mable asked.

"We need to confirm if he is Dylan's son," Finley said.

"I agree. It is the first step," Nestor said.

"How do you do that? DNA test?" I asked.

We all looked at Dylan. He shrugged, "I guess."

"Moonshine," I said. Dylan's eyes widened. Nestor flinched in his chair. "What?"

"I'm sorry. Go ahead," Dylan said.

"I have a recipe for homebrew. It's actually absinthe. I think there is a field here somewhere that has all the ingredients. Remember that explosion we were in a while back?" I asked Dylan.

"Yeah, Grace, I remember. Do you remember it?" he asked.

"Well, up until the part everything exploded. I made that absinthe, didn't I?" I asked. The memory seemed foggy.

"Yes, you did," Dylan breathed hard. I could practically hear his heart pounding.

"What is wrong with you?" I asked.

"You were hurt that day. It scared the crap out of me," he said.

I tried to focus on the house. Knowing I'd made the absinthe wasn't all there was to the story, but I couldn't remember. I knew that I hit my head pretty hard with the impact of the explosion. I remembered running from the house with Dylan, then nothing. I barely remembered being in the house other than to cook up the brew. It had a truth spell on it. For some reason, I wanted Dylan to drink it.

"Anyway. I could make up some, and we could make her drink it," I said.

Dylan shook his head. "You blew up one house. We aren't doing that again."

Troy came into the bar soaking wet.

"Dylan," he said. We all turned to look at him. It must have been pouring outside.

"What's wrong?" Dylan asked.

"She got to talking, and I had to go check, but it's true," he said.

"What's true?" I asked.

"The house is back," he said.

"My house?" Dylan asked jumping to his feet.

"Yeah, it's sitting out there like it never moved, but there is a ward around it. I couldn't get close to it," he said.

"She took my house!" Dylan fussed.

"Was there any doubt of that?" I asked.

He shook his head. "What else is she saying?"

"She says Grace will kill her, but she won't kill a kid. She said that's all that matters. She wanted him to be safe," Troy said.

"What's his name?" I asked. They all stared at me. "What?"

"Devin," Dylan replied.

"Faun" I said.

"What?" Dylan asked.

"Devin is a modern form of the old Irish family name that means faun," I said. "I bet his father is a faun."

"That's a Seelie fairy," Nestor said. I nodded in the affirmative.

"How did you know that?" Finley asked raising an eyebrow.

"I know lots of things little brother," I said. "Plus, Daddy's power helps."

"You cheat!" he proclaimed. A snicker circled the table.

"Look. I know I put on a big show in here earlier, but Levi pointed out that the council banished her. Something inside of me clicked. If it hadn't been for Levi, they both might be dead right now. We need to be careful who we banish from Shady Grove," I said. "We gave the council authority, and as long as I hold my father's power, it's the executive branch. I didn't realize that included executions."

"Even more reason to get that protection spell going," Mable added.

"Agreed. Finley, find Levi and set it up. If we need anything from the vault, use it. Okay?" I said. He nodded then trotted off out the door. "Betty, if you and Luther don't mind, could you drop by the diner and whip up some food for Stephanie and Devin. I don't really care about her, but the boy needs food."

"Sure thing, honey," Betty said. She stood up, patted Dylan on the back, and dragged Luther out the front door.

"I'll be upstairs," Mable said, dismissing herself.

Nestor looked at Dylan and me. "Do you really think the child isn't Dylan's?"

I grimaced, "I don't know. He's definitely fairy. I looked as I walked out the door with Levi. Faun makes sense. Do we have any fauns here?" I asked. Dylan squeezed my hand, remaining silent. He was overwhelmed. I squeezed back.

"Not that I know of," Nestor said. "Most of the fauns are in Rhiannon's army."

"Grace," Dylan whispered in my ear. "Can we please go home?"

I looked at his sad eyes. We needed to go home for the quiet. So many times, he had to assure me that he was here for me. That he wouldn't leave. He needed that from me now. I couldn't imagine my life without him, so it wasn't a stretch. It was like we were stuck ducks in a dry pond. There wasn't any way of getting out of this. We had to make do.

"Of course, let's get going," I said. "Goodnight, Nestor."

Dylan handed me the keys before crawling up in the passenger side of the truck. With a hop, skip and a jump, we were home at the trailer. He crawled out of the truck, in the same manner, as he had crawled into it. I followed him inside. He went straight to the fridge, grabbing a beer. He had it guzzled before I shut the door, then opened a second.

"Dylan," I said. "There is no need for that."

"I need to get drunk. Let me," he said.

"You've been drinking a lot lately," I said. "What's stressing you out?"

"I didn't think you noticed," he said.

"When are you going to learn that I notice everything, I just don't talk about it. Like tonight. I saw those looks you and Nestor passed around the table like it was Thanksgiving dinner. We were talking about the absinthe. More happened that day that I don't remember, but Dylan, I trust you. My outrage at Stephanie had nothing to do with my confidence in us. It had everything to do with the fact that she is meaner than a wet panther," I said.

He plopped down in the recliner. I walked over to him. He held his empty hand up to me, when I clasped his, he pulled me down on his lap. "This messes everything up," he said.

"Does it? You told me on our picnic the other day that you'd love me forever even if we never had a child. Has that changed?" I asked.

"No," he said. "I admit I was an idiot before we were together."

"Remember the night you arrested me?" I asked.

"Yeah," he said.

"I was being an idiot then, too. I did it pretty often," I said. "I probably still do it on the regular."

He smiled because he knew I was right. I didn't know whether to be mad at him or kiss him. I opted for the kiss. We would make it through this like everything else. "I'm tired, Glory," he said.

"Me too, Darlin'," I said.

"Come to bed with me," he said.

"I'd go off the edge of the earth with you," I said.

"Just the bed tonight," he said, as I slid off his lap. I pulled him up out of the chair.

We curled up in the bed together. His beer breath on the back of my neck. Usually, I would have made him gargle or something, but tonight it didn't matter. He needed to know that I loved him, beer breath and all.

CHAPTER SIX

WE STOOD LOOKING DOWN THE LANE AT THE HOUSE WE USED TO live in together. The restored antebellum stood proudly where it had before Stephanie took it. I could feel the ward reverberating around it. Dylan tried it out, and of course, it let him through, but not me. It didn't matter. Neither one of us was going into that house as long as Stephanie controlled it. We had our first Christmas together in that house. The memories of that day floated around in my mind.

Dylan had woken up irritated and moody. I decided to shut up and be supportive. Shocker. I was doing good with the supportive part. The other part, not so much.

"Can I kill her yet?" I asked.

"Be my guest," he muttered.

"Talk to me," I urged.

He kicked a rock at his feet, grumbling under his breath. I tried not to sigh, but I did. He grumbled some more. "I should go see my son," he said.

"Okay. Let's go," I said.

"You don't have to go, Grace," he said.

"I will behave. I promise," I said.

"It's not that. I just feel like you deserve better than this. You always have, and I've been nothing but a fuck up since day one," he said.

"What are you talking about?" I asked. "You've been a wonderful sheriff for this town. We did a lot of good together. We are still good together."

He opened his mouth to say something else, but instead, he walked back to the truck. He was driving today. I was just along for the ride.

We pulled up outside the Cabaha Motel. Amanda Capps sat in a cruiser with her son, Mark. They were eating biscuits. She waved at us when we arrived. I got out of the truck with Dylan, as a fine mist of rain fell. We ducked under the small awning over the door, and Dylan knocked.

"Come in," Stephanie's voice called out.

Dylan opened the door, and we both stepped in. Devin took one look at me, then ran into the bathroom. Stephanie scowled at me. "Did you come to kill me, Grace?" she asked.

"No," I replied. I leaned back on the door, forcing myself to remain quiet.

"Good morning, Dylan. What can I do for you?" she asked.

"I just hoped to talk to the boy," he said.

"Why? You don't think he is yours. He's terrified of Grace. I warned him that she was a wild card in all of this. She could strike us down with a snap of her fingers," she said.

"I'm pretty sure she wouldn't even have to snap," Dylan said. Stephanie showed just a moment of surprise but then went back to the haughty aloof face. She looked like a hundred years of bad facelifts. I wasn't sure what she was doing to her glamour, but it sucked. I decided I didn't want to look past it. "Stephanie, tell the truth. Is he really mine?"

"Sure. Remember the hot sex we had after the moonshine incident. I got pregnant. I slipped away to my mother's realm, had the child, then left him there. Brock found out about him and wanted to kill him, so I brought him here. Grace can't resist taking in other people's kids, since she can't seem to have one of her own," she said.

I didn't move. I didn't open my mouth. Dylan flinched but tilted his head sideways when I didn't. "I remember that you told me that you fucked Krykos that day plus someone else," he said, turning back to her.

"He looks just like you, Dylan," she said.

"You fucked Joey Blankenship, too," Dylan said. I knew that Joey looked just like Dylan.

"You want proof?" she asked.

"Yes," he said.

"Bond with him as your heir. If he isn't your blood, the bond won't transfer," she said.

I cleared my throat. Stephanie laughed.

"I never thought I'd see the day when you were tamed, Grace. It's impressive, Dylan," she said.

"Could you please ask the boy to come out?" Dylan said, ignoring her taunts. I was busting at the seams, but I had promised to behave.

"Devin, come out here and see your father. He is the reason we are here," she called out to him.

"No. The evil fairy is here," he said.

I touched Dylan on the arm. "I'll wait outside," I said softly.

"No, you don't have to," he said. I kissed him on the cheek then stepped outside into the light mist. Amanda waved me over to the cruiser. It was one of the ones without the dividing window. Her son crawled into the back, as I sat down in the passenger seat.

"How's it going in there?" she asked.

"I'm not sure. He's afraid of me, but Dylan wants to talk to him. I decided it might be better if I waited out here. She's obsessed with trying to provoke me," I said.

Amanda and I never really got along very well, but we tolerated each other since that night I tried to kill her. I supposed I should be thankful she even spoke to me. However, she was with Troy now and they seemed to be settled. I looked over at her, noticing the flashing diamond on her finger.

"He proposed?" I asked.

She smiled wide. "Yeah," she said. "We were going to tell everyone last night, but things got crazy."

"Congratulations!" I said. I meant it. I surprised myself that I meant it.

"Thank you. That means a lot coming from you," she said. "What if the kid is his?"

"Then it's his. We are still together. I can't live without him," I said.

She hummed for a moment, then turned silent. I listened to the rain pick up on the car's roof. Mark leaned over the seat looking at me.

"Hello, Mark," I said.

"Hi. Where's Winnie?" he asked.

"She's staying with her Aunt Tabitha today," I said.

"Oh," he said with a disappointed tone.

"You play with her at school?" I asked.

"Yep, but I want to go to her house. She says she has two fairies," he said.

"What?!" I asked.

"Yeah, she said she has two brownies that clean her room and play with her. I want to meet them," he explained. Amanda looked at me bewildered.

I buried my head in my hands. "She wasn't supposed to tell," I muttered.

Amanda laughed. "She's six. They don't understand secrets," she said.

"I know. I just hope that none of the regular kids found out," I said.

"No, she only told me, because we are best friends," he said, proudly.

I shrugged. There was nothing I could do at this point. Everyone in this town was fairy aware, so it wasn't a huge deal like it used to be, but it was a reminder that we needed to shut the town off from the rest of the world.

Dylan ducked out of the motel room, then made his way to the truck. I hurried out of the car, waving to Amanda. The bottom fell out just as I closed my door. Lightning ripped across the sky, and thunder shook the truck.

He didn't speak as he slammed the truck in reverse, speeding off down the road toward the trailer. When we got there, he high-tailed it into the house. I followed him in and found Levi and Finley sitting in the living room.

"Hey," Levi said.

I held my finger up, then followed Dylan into the bedroom. He slammed his fist into the wall. "Dylan!" I said, mostly because it startled me.

"He's a good kid. He needs a father," he said, rubbing his knuckles. He looked at me. "She wants me to bond with him, but I get the feeling it's a trap. A setup."

"Your instincts are usually right," I affirmed, waving my hand over the cuts on his knuckle. They disappeared.

"You have a lot of power you don't show," he said.

"A lot," I said. "Like super-duper scary lot."

He smiled at my nonsense, then wrapped me in a big hug. "I love you, Grace. I can't do this without you."

"I'm here," I said.

"Go see what those two knuckleheads want. I'll be out in a minute," he said, planting a kiss on my forehead. When he released me, I stumbled backward almost losing my balance. He grabbed me to steady me. My head spun for a moment. "Whoa! Sorry!"

"No. I can't seem to stand on my own two feet," I said giggling.

He leaned into my ear. "Does that mean you want to lay on the bed?"

"Not with my brother and bard in the next room," I said.

"Right," he smiled. I could tell he felt better. "Go. If you can walk."

"Hey!" I protested.

"They say in your old age you revert to your childhood," he grinned.

I opened my mouth wide, but I had no response. I just wanted to kick his ass.

"It's rude to talk about a woman's age," Levi said from the other room.

I cocked my head sideways and tried to hold back a grin.

"Shut up, Levi," Dylan said.

When I walked into the room, Levi and Finley acted like they had heard nothing from the other room. Levi was explaining college football to Finley who had no idea about the concept.

"It's not even August, Levi," I said.

"Doesn't matter. Texas will be back this season," he said confidently.

"Texas had to be somewhere in the first place to be back," Dylan called from the other room.

Normal. I liked normal.

"Y'all want something to drink?" I asked.

"Do you have sweet tea?" Finley asked. Sweet tea was not something I kept in my house. I never acquired the taste of it and received many beatdowns from my fellow southerners for my lack of taste. But when I opened the fridge, a large jug of sweet tea sat there.

"Dylan, did you buy tea?" I asked.

"No, why?" he said, joining me in the kitchen. He looked in the fridge because he knew I didn't drink it. He did, but he usually picked it up at the diner.

"*Trying something new. Did it work?*" Levi's voice echoed in my head. I teetered again like I did in the bedroom.

"Grace, you need to sit down," Dylan said, grabbing me again.

"Damn it, Dublin. Get out of my head. Yes, there is tea here," I said rubbing my temples.

Dylan shot him an evil look. I hadn't heard Levi in my head since just before Finley took me to see the vault.

"Tea it is," I said, gently pushing Dylan away. He took the jug before I could grab it. It was my cue to go sit down.

"Did it hurt? It's never hurt you before. Are you feeling okay?" Levi asked. His face was filled with concern. His voice had been loud before, but I had never lost my balance.

"No. Just rattled around a bit," I said, staring at Finley to get out of the recliner.

"Oh!" he said, jumping up. He joined Levi on the couch. They sat on opposite ends.

"Sorry," Levi mumbled.

"Don't worry. I'm fine."

He sighed, leaning back in the chair.

"Why are you here?" I asked out loud.

"We have everything ready for the concealment spell for the town. Mayor Jenkins said he got the okay from Judge Chastain. Apparently, the water in Shady Grove has gone toxic, forcing all the residents to relocate. We should do it at night to avoid any suspicion," Finley said. Finley was good at the politics side of things. He told me that when he wasn't looking after me in the real world, he was in court with father. He said that he learned a lot about ruling. I had already decided that he should rule the Otherworld instead of me, but I hadn't told him that just yet. It was painfully obvious that we had to take back my father's kingdom. He and I actually talked strategy. Dylan helped sometimes, too. We needed a lot more support, but I didn't know where that support would come from. I could walk in there and claim it, but that didn't mean that it would automatically be mine. Finley said there would be many challenges. Some just to acknowledge my rule, but the others would be real. I would have to fight. Or choose a champion to fight for me.

I didn't tell them, for fear it would hurt their manly egos, but Levi was the most powerful among them. Finley had a natural fighting instinct, and Dylan was like a five-star recruit. But the sheer power that Levi possessed staggered even me. He felt it too. He feared it. No matter how much I pushed, he only dabbled in it. I couldn't fault him. I had been doing the same thing. However, it was time to jump in the power pool. Stephanie's arrival cemented that thought in my head.

It was time to be a Queen.

"What the hell are you dreaming about?" Finley asked, smirking at me.

"None of your business," I replied.

"Me," Dylan interjected. Instead of sitting with me in the recliner, he pulled up a chair next to me.

Queen, be a queen.

Bah. Who was I kidding? A real fairy queen would have Finley guarding the door while I fucked both Levi and Dylan. Levi grunted. I raised my eyebrows at him. He blushed. Holy shit. Time to block my thoughts.

"*Good idea,*" he said.

"What was that?" Dylan said, not missing a beat.

"My mind wandered," I said. "I'll explain later so Levi doesn't bust a nut over there."

Finley laughed, then punched him in the arm. "What about the kid?" Finley asked. "Is he yours?"

"Don't know. Stephanie wants me to try to bond with him," Dylan said.

"What does that entail?" Levi asked.

"He has to share his fire with him. If the fire moves to the kid, then he's his heir. If the fire burns him, then he's not," I said.

Dylan stared at me. "How did you know that?"

"Daddy," I mumbled.

"His knowledge or you talked to him?" he asked.

"Knowledge. It seems that I can access a lot more of it," I said.

"You are accepting it," Finley said.

I nodded. Queen. Be a queen. "Call Tabitha and see if she can keep Winnie for one more night," I said.

"Woohoo!" a shout came from Winnie's room.

"Fucking brownies," Levi said.

"All the time," I said. "I had to put a dampener spell up to drown out the thrusting and grunts. Who knew two little things could make so much noise?"

"I wondered what that spell was when I saw it," Levi said.

I was happy that he was even looking for such things. He probably felt it when he came into the trailer. I only put it up when Winnie was away, because for the most part Bramble and Briar kept their sexual exploits to times when Winnie wasn't here. However, I was well-aware of the fairy sex drive. If I ever caught them doing it with her around, both of them would be out on their asses.

"I'll call," Dylan said, taking his phone out of his pocket.

CHAPTER SEVEN

Finley and Dylan went to all the entrances into town from the other parts of the state. They had signs made saying that the town was closed. Troy worked with state officials sent by Judge Chastain to move the Sheriff's department to another city. They had built a new jail in Sarasota which was about twelve miles from Shady Grove. Almost all of the department would be moving there. Except for the few that were on the force that were fairies or Lycans. Troy kept those he trusted, and we would form our own Shady Grove Police Department. Dylan and he would be in charge together. Dylan insisted on having Troy as an equal partner because of his connection with me. He didn't want anyone to think he was biased which made me laugh, because I knew if anyone opposed me it would be him.

I made a quick trip to town stopping by the diner for some lunch, and then by Hot Tin to talk to Nestor. He knew I'd want to talk to him alone after everything that happened the night before.

"So, the house is sitting there like it never moved?" he asked.

"Yeah. It brought back memories," I said.

"It was a good Christmas," he said. "The best I'd ever had."

I smiled because it was the only Christmas we had all spent

together as a family. It meant the world to me. It saddened me, even more, to think about the rainbow room that Dylan had made for Winnie in the house. It was almost like he knew before we ever got together that she would be our child. I didn't think that premonition or foresight was an ability of a phoenix, but perhaps it was.

"I don't know what to do," I said.

"About the child?" he asked.

I nodded as tears began to flow. He sighed, offering me his towel. I blotted the tears, trying to find the right words to say. "Is it selfish of me to hate the fact that she got to give him a child and I didn't? It should have been me," I said. "it's like all those years we worked together, I could have pursued him if I hadn't been so afraid of Jeremiah and the Sanhedrin. We had a connection, but I ignored it."

"Grace, you and Dylan have always been connected. You never ignored it. Neither did he, but Jeremiah forcefully kept the two of you apart. I believe he was angry at Dylan for choosing Stephanie in the first place. Dylan knew very early on it was a mistake, but by then he was in too deep. There are still many things that you don't know. It's not my place to tell them, but one day you will know. It will help you understand it all. In the meantime, let's operate on the idea that Devin is not Dylan's son. Okay?" Nestor said.

I pondered his words. Nestor just skimmed over information that I didn't know. More things that were hidden from me, but he was right. I had to truly believe that Devin wasn't Dylan's son. It was my only hope of getting through this. I can't imagine what my state of mind might be if it turned out that he *was* Dylan's son.

"Okay," I said.

"How's the set up going for the concealment?" he asked.

"Hopefully, very well. I saw something about it on the news, but the state troopers came in to make sure no reporters tried to get into the city. Once we have the spell up, they won't be able to see anything anyway. Provided that the spell works. It's all dependent upon Levi remembering the spell correctly from the book," I said.

"Why was there a spell like that in the book?" he asked.

"Black Death," I said.

"Oh, for a quarantine?" he asked.

"Yes. Taliesin hid a city that was free of the plague so that people would have a safe haven. Mostly fairies. From what I understand, the disease spread quickly. Even through the fairy population," I explained.

"I remember. It was devastating on the exiles at the time. We hid out the best we could from it," he said. "I had to move several times as it swept through Europe."

"I was with a band of Roma then. It was hard on them as well. Thankfully, I never got it," I said.

"As a matter of fact, she nursed most of us back to health. The plague never touched her," a voice said behind me.

When I turned around, a young man from my earlier days stood before me. My mouth fell open in shock as I looked at his features. He hadn't changed a bit from the time I knew him. Pale green eyes and dark hair falling in waves around his head under a large black hat. Beaded necklaces hung around his neck, and leather bracelets adorned both arms. The white shirt he wore opened in the middle revealing dark caramel skinned chest and black hairs.

"Fordele," I whispered.

"Hannah," he said smiling.

"By the gods, you *are* alive. Finley said you were, but I didn't believe it," I said, standing up from my stool. A grin stretched across his face, as he took three quick steps to me. He wrapped his arms around my shoulders. He stood almost six and a half feet tall.

"Hello, beautiful woman," he said. I pushed away from him gently. "Sorry. I know that you are taken. I am as well. My wife Wendy is outside with the rest of our group."

"Gypsies? You brought them here?" I asked.

"Yes. Word has spread through all this country and the old one about Shady Grove, and its Queen," he said, lifting my chin to look him in the eyes.

"I'm sorry for what happened," I said.

"It was a long time ago. I hated you for it, but no longer. To hold that sort of anger for twenty lifetimes is even more than I could bear. You ran because you were afraid."

"I ran because I saw them take you. I knew they would kill you," I said.

"Funny thing that," he said. "They intended to use me as bait for you. It was a good thing you ran."

"They finally caught up with me," I said.

"But here you are," he said.

"Here I am," I replied.

"Come meet my wife," he said, holding his hand out to me. He looked up to Nestor for the first time. "Do you mind if I take her for a moment?"

"Ford, this is Nestor, my grandfather," I said.

"Oh, I thought he looked a little old for your tastes," he said.

I giggled. "No, he's a little too much kin for my tastes."

"I hear they do that kind of thing in this place," he said.

"Vicious rumors," I said. "Don't confuse Alabama with Mississippi."

I followed him into the parking lot of Hot Tin. It was filled with station wagons. They were painted in various bright colors with tassels hanging from their antennas. Ford led me to a Volvo V90 by which a beautiful, tall woman stood. Her long colorful dress sparkled in the sunlight. The golden jewelry she wore hung down around her neck and ears in cascades. A large ornate ring was attached from the inside of her nose to the outside with small dangly bits hanging from it. A smile spread across her face.

"Oh, you must be Hannah!" she said, embracing me tightly. I'd forgotten how handsy the gypsy people were. I felt the tingle of power when she touched me.

"Grace. I go by Grace now," I said. "It's a pleasure to meet you."

"Wendy," she said smiling. The Volvo boasted a large, magnetic sign on the side that said Wendy's Fortunes and Fates.

"Fortune teller?" I asked.

"Yes," she replied as Ford hooked his arm around her waist. He smiled broadly, kissing her on the forehead.

"Are you a real seer?" I asked.

She blushed, "I am. It is why we are here."

"You brought them to Shady Grove?" I asked.

"Yes, I foresaw a time in the near future when our kind will be hunted. We will be safe here, with your permission, of course," she said.

"Of course. I see no reason you all can't stay here," I said.

"Be sure you know there are close to one hundred of us," he said.

"Oh, wow!" I said. "We've had an exodus of humans leaving, so I'm pretty sure there will be plenty of room here for all of you. There is a council, but I doubt any of them will object. Well, I take that back. They might, but frankly, I'm the deciding vote."

"We have a bad reputation, you know?" Ford said.

"Ford, I used to live with you guys. I have all the bad reputation this town can handle. I doubt any of you can match it," I said. They laughed. Ford knew it was true.

"We will stay, for now," he said.

"You are travelers. I know that, but you are welcome here as long as I have a say in things," I said. Dylan pulled up in a plain black four-door car. I supposed he had turned in his cruiser to the county. He walked up to me, put his arm around me matching Ford's stance, and said, "Howdy folks."

"Hello, I'm Fordele," Ford said, offering a hand to Dylan.

Dylan shook it. "The Fordele?" he asked looking at me.

I blushed. "Yes. Ford, this is Dylan. My fiancé."

"Well, congrats to you, Dylan. She is a fine woman," Ford said.

"Now we both get to have exes in town," Dylan grinned, knowing full well that Remy lived here part of the time.

"Ugh," I said. "Don't mention it."

"Welcome to Shady Grove. May I talk to you a moment?" Dylan asked.

"Sure. Please excuse me," I said.

Dylan held my hand as we walked back toward the black car he arrived in. "Everything is set up for tonight. We've done a sweep. None of the humans that were here except Cletus and Tater, remain," he said.

"Good. Have you spoken to Finley and Levi?" I asked.

"No, but we will hit them up in a minute. So, Fordele, huh?" he said looking over my shoulder at the gypsy man whispering in his wife's ear.

"Yeah, he came in the bar when I was talking to Nestor," I said.

"What's that like seeing him after so long?" he asked.

"Weird. Very weird," I said.

"No lingering feelings?" he asked. I shot him a look but realized he was playing. I pinched him hard in the side. "Damn, Grace, that hurts."

"No. The only feeling I felt was, oh shit, I left him to die. He's here for revenge," I said.

"Well, I suppose that's a possibility," he said. "He would have to go through me."

"Where do we send them to set up?" I asked, ignoring the testosterone.

"Probably down to the ballpark, you think?" he asked.

"Yeah, that sounds good," I replied. When I looked up, Nestor stood in the doorway of the bar surveying the newest additions to Shady Grove.

"Wow. So many of them," he said.

I sighed. More people for me to protect. Be a queen. My new mantra rattled around in my head. I didn't know what to think of myself, but it didn't matter at this point. I asked for all of it, or rather, accepted it with a nudge from my fiancé. He took that moment to press his body into my back, wrapping his arms around my waist. His breath tickled my neck.

"Don't worry. You've got this," he said.

I didn't respond, except to lean back into him. Troy pulled up in another black car. Approaching us, he took off his sunglasses and stared at the spectacle.

"Gypsies?" he asked.

"Yeah, can you lead them down to the ballpark to set up camp? If they want houses, we will have to coordinate that with the council. I think Betty is in charge of housing," I said.

"Sure thing. The perimeter is set for when we start the ritual," he replied.

"Thanks, Troy. Oh, and congratulations," I said.

He blushed, "Thanks, Grace. That means a lot."

"Congratulations for what?" Dylan asked.

"He asked Amanda to marry him," I said.

"Well, I'll be damned. Troy, when were you going to tell me?" Dylan shouted out to him.

Troy laughed, "I didn't tell anyone. Amanda must have told."

"I saw the ring," I said. "Kinda obvious."

"While I was in the motel?" he asked as his voice turned less jovial.

"Yes," I said quietly.

He kissed the space just below my ear on my neck sending a shiver down my spine. "Oh, good spot?" he asked.

"Hmm, yes," I said.

"I went by there earlier. He's talking to me a little more, but I'm still not convinced he is mine," he said. "Something in the way he responds. It seems like Stephanie has coached him on what to say to me."

I didn't respond again. Perhaps holding my tongue was the best new trick I could learn. My heart hurt knowing that that child was in this town and there wasn't a damn thing I could do about it. The council would meet tonight after the ritual to take any questions about the concealment spell. We could all talk about Stephanie's fate then. But for the moment, I had to endure the thought that a hateful woman had taken away all my dreams for Dylan and me.

CHAPTER EIGHT

As I waited for Levi to join me at the trailer, I paced around the room. Rufus watched me from the recliner. It had become his spot, and he would groan anytime I asked him to move. Silly dog. Dylan went with the other officers to double check the perimeter for the ritual. We were all in touch via walkie-talkies that the state gave Troy to use in Shady Grove. I wondered how many state officials knew exactly what was going on in our little town.

Levi came in with the darkest look on his face that I had ever seen.

"Someone take your favorite toy, Levi?" I asked.

He pressed his lips together, shaking his head. "No, let's just go. I'm on the Harley. Just so you know," he replied.

"I'll drive the truck," I said.

"You can't trust me even now? There are hardly any vehicles in this town. Why can't you just ride with me?" he fussed.

Pressing my hand on his cheek, he shuddered at the tingle between us. It was still strong with physical contact. "What's wrong?"

"I can't talk about it," he said.

Disappointment broke my heart. "Okay," I mumbled, then

turned to the bedroom to grab my jacket. His strong arms wrapped around my waist, pulling me back to him.

His voice floated through my head like a lover's song.

"*Dylan knows this is his child. I just have a gut feeling about it, Grace. He's playing you for a fool in front of everyone. It hurts me to see you buy into it because you are blinded by your love for him. I don't want to see you hurt anymore. He's had so many chances to get this right, and he can't seem to do it.*"

"*Levi, you are wrong. It's not his child. I have a gut feeling too. The child on the outside looks a lot like Dylan, but on the inside, his aura is so far removed from Dylan's that they cannot be related. Stephanie is playing us all,*" I said. "*I love you for looking out for me, but this is going to work out.*"

"*I can't stand by and watch him tear you apart,*" he said.

I jerked away from him as tears formed in my eyes. "Then maybe you should leave Shady Grove, Levi. I have no desire to torture you. Perhaps I should have let you go last night," I said.

"That isn't what I want," he said.

"Is it not? You asked for it, or did you forget that?" I asked.

"No, I didn't forget, but that was before his past walked through that door ripping your heart out," he said. "I could feel it, or did you forget that I could feel it because I'm connected to it?"

"We have a ritual to do. This can wait," I said.

"It really can't wait, but I'll do whatever you want," he said.

"Good. I'm grabbing my jacket. I'll meet you outside," I replied.

He skulked out the door. I looked down at Rufus who hadn't budged from the recliner. Grabbing my leather jacket, I got a whiff of musk and peppermint. I'd told Dylan that my jacket didn't smell like his, so apparently, he sprayed his cologne on it. I felt something in the pocket. I pulled it out to find a piece of peppermint with a tiny note. "Now it smells right. Love you."

Levi was wrong.

~

LEVI and I pulled up outside the edge of town at the northernmost point. The road we were on traveled between town and the interstate. Nestor and Dylan waited for us there. I walked up, giving him a big hug.

"What's that for?" he asked.

"Peppermint," I said, handing him the piece from my jacket pocket. He grinned, and I melted all over again. He gave me a quick kiss while Nestor stood by smiling at us.

"Let's get married," Dylan said.

"We are getting married," I replied.

"No, as soon as possible. I don't want to wait," he said.

"Okay. I'll talk to Tabitha, and we can see how quickly we can put it together," I replied.

"Really?" he responded excitedly.

"Sure. Why not?" I said as he picked me up in a huge hug.

"Thank you, Grace," he said.

"Don't be silly. Alright, Levi. Let's do this. What do we need to do?" I asked.

Levi strummed his guitar lightly making sure it was in tune. "It's going to take a while, but I need you and Nestor to stand in the middle of the road and hold hands. I will start with Nestor to make the circuit around town. I will have to go to every major entrance to town while playing the song. Thankfully, I don't have to walk through the woods. Dylan will drive your truck, and I'll sit in the back playing. Just take it easy over the potholes," he said. "It might take a couple of hours, but you need to hold hands the entire time. You guys are the beginning and end of the spell."

"Okay. Can we sit?" I asked.

"No, standing is what the book said. When they did it in the book for the plague, it was a much smaller town. I'm just hoping it works for such a large area," he said.

"It will work. Size doesn't matter," I said.

Dylan choked, then coughed. Levi blushed, and Nestor laughed at them both.

"Men," I muttered.

"Love you," Dylan said, kissing me on the cheek. I gave him the keys to the truck, as he dropped the tailgate for Levi to ride in the back.

"Love you, too. See you soon," I said.

Joining hands with Nestor, we stood in the center of the road. Perhaps we should have had someone here with us to make sure no one ran us over but we stood inside the barricades that the state had erected. Thankfully, there were no reporters or lookie-loos. Levi pressed his back to Nestor's side. I felt the magic swirl around us as he prepared himself to play. Despite our conversation in the trailer, I was so proud of him at this moment. He had confidence that he could do this for the town.

"*I am so proud you, Levi. I know you can do this,*" I said giving him just a little support.

"*Thanks, Grace,*" he responded with a hint of irritation. I was used to his constant state of distress. We did need to find some way to make him happy, and unlike when he first moved here, there wasn't a woman who could satisfy him. Not anymore.

Looking through my fairy sight, I watched as he strummed the first note. The sound reverberated through the magical spectrum lighting it up in a thousand different colors like a rippling rainbow. It reminded me of the walls of Mike's Magic Vape shop. Levi's song sounded like home to me. Something comforting and worth protecting. It was perfect for the task. As he walked slowly away from Nestor to the back of the truck, a wave of magic followed behind him. Dylan let the step down on the tailgate, and Levi easily climbed into the bed of the truck while playing constantly. I hoped his fingers were up to this. Dylan got in the truck with a wave to us and pulled out. Levi stood against the cab, balancing and playing at the same time. I watched the ribbon of magic follow him down the road.

"You watching it?" Nestor asked.

"Yes, it's mesmerizing," I replied.

"He's very powerful," Nestor said.

"I know," I replied. "He's mad at me for believing Dylan."

"He's not mad at you. He's frustrated with the situation and doesn't know how to handle it other than to be angry."

"How do we handle it?" I asked.

"Your father's answer was to please all of those who loved him, but I know that isn't your way. But perhaps Levi needs something that is just yours and his, something meaningful that he can find happiness in. I think Dylan would tolerate it if it took pressure off of you. I know that Levi's attitude is starting to wear on your sensibilities. He's important to you, and to all of us. Should you ever lose control, and I'm not saying you will, Levi is our one defense," he said.

"Dylan can calm me as well," I said.

"Not like Levi," he said.

I watched as the ribbon changed directions. It stretched now into the tree-line to our right, snapping into place as Levi made the first connection to Betty who was just west of us on the next town entry point. At each point, a prominent town member stood waiting for Levi to connect them to the rest. When he was done, he would close the circle with me. So far it seemed to be working.

Considering Nestor's words, I tried to think of something that Levi and I could share that would just be ours. It still concerned me that I would have something that Dylan and I couldn't share. I would definitely see what he thought about it before doing anything. He was my heart and soul now. I couldn't hide anything from him.

An hour went by as we waited. I felt the power growing in the center of the circle. My legs started to get tired, and I shifted my weight several times. Nestor looked tired as well.

"You okay?" he asked.

"Yeah. Just feel a little woozy," I said. I released power from my tattoo letting it course over both of us. Nestor sighed as the power comforted our aches. "Better?"

"Yes. Thank you, Child," he said. I twisted my lips to him calling me, *Child*, but I let it go. He was my elder after all. "How's the boy?"

"I haven't seen him since yesterday. Dylan visited him twice today to make sure they had everything they needed. He said Stephanie is just biding her time waiting for him to bond with the boy," I said.

"That's a bad idea," Nestor said.

"He said his instinct is that it is a trap. She probably has some sort of spell on the kid that will make it look like Devin is Dylan's son," I said.

"Knowing that, you could use it to your advantage. Let Dylan do the bonding. If it is his child, then it needed to be done either way. But if it isn't, then no harm, but we get to see what Stephanie's motive is behind all of this. It seems strange that she would just leave Brock after all this time. Surely, he knew about the child since he was born in the Otherworld," Nestor said.

I cringed at the thought, and the wooziness returned to my head. My knees were locked, and I started to wobble. The sound of my truck approaching broke me out of the daze. I saw the ribbon of power approaching us. It stretched out toward the east where it was connected to Mayor Jenkins. Dylan pulled the truck sideways in the road so that Levi could get to me faster. He looked tired, but the song didn't waiver. I saw blood dripping from his fingers.

"Levi!" I called out. Nestor gripped my hand tightly, keeping me in place.

Dylan held his hand out. "He's fine, Grace. Stay there. It's almost done."

Levi nodded slightly to me as he started to step off the tailgate of the truck. Dylan steadied him so that he could continue to play. Levi approached me with the ribbon of power following him. He walked straight up to my side pressing his body against mine and finishing the song. The circle snapped up between Nestor and me. I could see the circle completed through our joined hands.

"Everyone, hold your position," Dylan said into his walkie.

"Now what?" I asked.

Levi released the guitar letting it hang around his shoulder. He looked through his sight at the circle joined at our hands. "Just let go. The circle will stay," he said.

He took a deep breath, and for just a moment, I felt his confidence waiver. Nestor looked at me because he must have felt it too. We released our hands, and immediately the circle fizzled.

"Fuck!" Levi said, swinging his guitar on the ground smashing it into shards of wood.

"Levi, it's okay," I tried to coax him.

"No, it's not! I did exactly what the book said," he growled.

He pounded the pavement with the broken guitar. He didn't stop until I touched his tattoo. When he slumped to his knees, I followed him to the ground. I coaxed him to let go of the shattered neck of the guitar. I called power to my hands lightly brushing against his to heal his bleeding fingers.

"It's okay. We will figure it out. It's my fault for letting the book go," I said.

"You let it go because you trusted me," he replied.

Nestor and Dylan stood back, allowing me to deal with Levi. I was thankful for it. Dylan turned down the radio as people began to ask what happened. He walked away from us, responding quietly.

"Everyone will know I failed," he said.

"No one will know. We will tell them that it was me. That I broke hands with Nestor or something. Let me take it," I said.

"No," he grumbled.

"As your Queen, I am responsible for you. That means accepting your victories as well as your setbacks. This isn't a defeat. We will figure it out," I said. "In fact, I might just send Finley after the book. You can go with him."

"Yes, let's do that," he said finally looking at me. His blue eyes had a light in them I hadn't seen in a while.

"*There's my bard,*" I said.

"*Thank you for not being angry at me about this. I thought you would go off on me after the way I've acted lately,*" he said.

"*I'm trying something new. More Queen-like,*" I said.

"*A real monarch would have killed me on the spot,*" he suggested.

"*I could never kill someone I love. My father didn't kill me. I won't harm you,*" I said.

"*I'm not your child,*" he grumbled.

"*No, I find you far too sexy to be my child,*" I said.

"*What?*" he said surprised.

"*I may be engaged, but I'm not blind, Levi,*" I said. That seemed to be all he needed to get up off the ground. He bounded up, offering his hand to help me. Nestor offered as well. I let both of them pull me up when I reached my feet the circle snapped back into place through Nestor's hand in mine. "What the hell?"

"I suppose we will just have to stand here," Nestor smiled.

"I suppose so," I laughed. "It's still there, Levi. We just need to find a way to anchor it. Right now, it's anchored to our grip."

"The book said the circle should stay even after the physical bond was broken," he said.

"What happens after that in the book?" I asked.

"Taliesin talks about how the town was safe from the plague, and that he along with a lot of exiled fairies stayed in the town until the threat of the plague went away. He describes the room he stayed in and the people in the town. Nothing else about the shield," Levi said.

"We will talk to Finley, and you guys can go after the book," I said.

"What?" Dylan said walking back up.

"We need the book," I said. "Levi and Finley can go to Summer and get it. Finley should be accepted as an emissary from my father's kingdom. Hopefully, Rhiannon won't imprison them. I'm pretty sure Finley could charm anyone."

Levi cleared his throat. I turned to him. "You stay away from her. She will ruin you," I said.

"You can't keep me for yourself, Grace," Levi grinned.

"Come on, let's get to town before there is a panic," I said ignoring him. Maybe I was keeping him to myself. He could have whatever girlfriend he wanted, but the Summer Queen better keep her hands off my bard.

CHAPTER NINE

"Riley is there, too," Dylan reminded me on our way to the community center.

"Yeah, but he's already been with her, so it's like it doesn't bother me," I said.

"She and Jeremiah manipulated us to get the book, Grace. That should bother you," he said.

"We are getting the book back, so it doesn't matter," I replied. "Levi has been itching to get out of town. Maybe this is what he needs."

"How is it going to affect you?" Dylan asked.

"It won't because I can stay in control. Besides, Mr. Phoenix knows how to break my chill," I replied playfully.

He shook his head. "I just think the separation will be more than you imagine it to be," he said.

Levi stood outside the building waiting for us. Dylan helped me out of the truck. My legs felt numb from standing so long with Nestor. He pulled up next to us in his small pickup truck with Mable.

"*It's not good,*" Levi said.

"*They don't scare me,*" I replied.

"You ready?" Dylan asked.

"As I'll ever be," I said as he took my hand.

Nestor, Mable, and Levi followed us into the room. Finley stood just inside the door. He nodded to us as we passed him. The volume of angry voices flashed against my face when we walked in the crowded auditorium. A wave of heat rolled around the room that was staggering. No one stopped shouting even as Dylan and I walked up the center aisle to the stage. Betty, Tabitha, and Diego Santiago sat in chairs on the stage. Winnie jumped out of Tabitha's lap, running to us. Dylan caught her up in his arms as she latched on to his neck.

"They are being so loud. They need to use their inside voices," Winnie said, holding on to Dylan.

"Mommy is going to make them be quiet," he said.

He and Levi climbed the steps to the stage with Nestor who took his seat representing the council. I allowed my glamour to fade as I made my way up the steps. Looking across the room, I realized the enormity of the task I'd agreed to take on. Shady Grove was only a population of about 1,400 people when I first moved to town. With the humans gone and our new additions, I beheld the exiles that now depended upon my protection. I didn't need to estimate how many there were. In this form, I knew there were 823 fairies in the room with 214 not here, because they were children, parents of children, Troy's police force monitoring the roads, and those who just chose not to be here. 1,037 fairies including the 104 gypsies that joined our town this afternoon. Fordele stood with Wendy in the back corner. His gypsies lined the walls watching the rabble curiously. They continued to shout angry words at each other and toward the council.

Centering myself on the stage, I muttered, "Be the Queen."

"Silence," I said in a normal tone of voice. The room became deathly quiet, except for a chuckle from the direction of the gypsies. "This evening, Levi completed the circle of protection around the town." Before I even finished, Diego started to speak. He hadn't so much as uttered a syllable when I turned on him. "You may speak when I allow you to speak. Are we clear?"

"Yes, my Queen," he replied.

"As I was saying, unfortunately, the protection is only in place as long as Nestor and I hold hands at the completion point. We will need to discover what kind of anchor is needed to tie the spell in place. If anyone has any insight on that matter, they may speak to me privately after this meeting. In the meantime, the new Shady Grove Police Department will handle patrolling the checkpoints. Those of you with magical inclinations will be drafted to create cantrip spells along the borders in the woods to alert us to anything that might be passing the safe zone. If you would like to volunteer to do that, please see Mable Sims. She will coordinate the placement and timing of those cantrips. Finally, I am sending my brother, Finley, along with Levi to Rhiannon's realm to retrieve the song-book. I take full responsibility for allowing it to leave our possession. I trusted my longtime friend, Jeremiah Freyman, and he has betrayed me. He will be dealt with accordingly. Finley and Levi will retrieve the book and return it to my possession. Just to add, because I know nothing is a secret in this town, Stephanie Davis has returned to town. The council will meet after this to decide her fate. I did not kill her immediately for which I'm grateful to Levi for stopping me. I have no desire to take a mother from a child especially in front of his face. If any of you have questions, tough. I'm not dealing with it tonight. Go to your homes. Be with your families. You are safe. We will start the cantrip process tomorrow. This meeting is adjourned."

I saw angry faces flaring across the room, but I had to defuse the situation. The last thing I needed was them to feed off each other's anger. Perhaps by dismissing them, they would go home and let it go. I supposed it could backfire to the point where they all got angrier after letting it simmer, but I knew I could deal with it better in smaller groups. Otherwise, I would have to unleash Levi on all of them which in hindsight might have been interesting.

"If anyone makes a move this way, I'm stopping them," Levi said. I saw him drawing power to himself. A large amount of it. Dylan felt it, looking back and forth between us.

"It's okay," I assured Dylan.

The crowd dispersed quickly, and no one made a move toward the stage. I was thankful until I saw the looks on the council's faces.

"You may speak," I said.

Diego rushed toward me, but Dylan was between us in an instant. His fist flamed as Diego's claws shot out of his paws. I didn't stop it. Diego fought me every chance he got, and frankly, I was tired of it. Diego stopped in his tracks half-shifted. His long arms were hairy with enormous paws, but they were attached to a human torso.

"Stand down, Diego," Dylan warned him. Finley approached him from the other side of the stage. His royal armor had appeared, and he stood with his sword in hand. It glowed with chilly blue light.

Levi approached slowly, but I held my hand out to him urging him to hold his magic. "Levi, take Winnie to Mable," I said. He scooped her up, rushing her to the door.

"All of you protect her. She isn't fit to lead us," he growled shaking his paw at me. His voice rumbled in the room.

"We will talk about this, but not with fists and claws," Dylan said.

"You are all fools. The true queen has returned. We should follow her instead," Diego said showing his true colors.

Laughter overtook me. I couldn't help myself. All this time, Diego Santiago was a Stephanie supporter. I should have known. "Do all the shifters agree with you? Or is this your personal opinion?" I asked from behind Dylan.

"He doesn't speak for all of us," Amanda said from the doorway who stood there with Levi. "I had a feeling he would show himself tonight. Troy said I should be here just in case."

"Oh, really. Are you planning a coup, Mr. Santiago?" I asked.

He looked at all of us, knowing he'd shown his hand. He was a traitor.

"Dylan," I said softly. He stepped away from me allowing me to look Diego in the eye. "Mr. Santiago, you have committed treason against the kingdom of the Exiles. Do you have anything to say in your defense?" I asked.

"I helped her get back in town. I wanted her here to show you how a real queen should be," he said.

"In accordance to his admission of guilt, I have the power to remove him from the council. Are there any objections?" I asked looking at the other council members. They shook their heads. "Very well. Diego Santiago, you are removed from your council seat. I propose Amanda Capps take his place out of sheer convenience. Council, please vote."

"Yes," Tabitha said.

"Yes," Nestor said.

"Shame on you, Diego. Yes," Betty said. I had to laugh. She loved to get her word in.

"Miss Capps, would you care to join us?" I asked.

"I would love to," she replied, stepping up on the stage. She sat down in Diego's seat.

"On your knees, Mr. Santiago," I said.

"No," he protested.

"I said, on your knees!" I forced my will out through my voice. The stage shook when the large man's knees hit the wooden planks.

I walked toward the kneeling man. "Levi, go outside and see if anyone is left in the parking lot. I'd like a few witnesses."

"Okay," he said with wide eyes. He knew what I intended to do. For a moment, my resolve wavered, but I had told myself I needed to be the queen. That included executions.

Levi hurried outside, returning with a few people from town including a couple of the gypsies. I looked into the pale green eyes of Fordele as he and his wife, Wendy, entered the back of the auditorium.

"Thank you all for joining us. Mr. Santiago has admitted to treason. I wanted there to be witnesses to the actions taken by the council and myself just in case there were any questions when word traveled tomorrow around town. Now, Mr. Santiago, did you help Stephanie Davis return to Shady Grove despite our banishment?" I asked.

"Yes," he replied defiantly.

"You did this knowing that the punishment for treason is death, correct?" I asked.

"Yes," he replied.

My eyes met Dylan's for a moment. I wanted to know what he thought of me. With a look, I knew that he supported me completely. A rush of confidence flowed over me as I turned to the council.

"As always, we vote," I said to the council. "Vote your conscious. If you want him to live, then he will be imprisoned for life. If you want him to suffer the consequences of his actions, then he will die."

"Death," Amanda said without hesitation.

"Death," Betty echoed.

Nestor rubbed his hand through his hair. I wouldn't be angry with him if he voted for him to live. Nestor was kinder than I would ever be. "He must die," Nestor said to my surprise.

"I agree," Tabitha finished.

Before anything else was said, I pulled power from my tattoo and snapped my fingers. Diego Santiago burst into a fine dust of ice and snow which melted before it even hit the floor. I'd seen my father do it numerous times. I didn't think. I just pulled on his wealth of knowledge and power to force myself to do it. I gasped after a moment, and Dylan looked alarmed.

"Shit," I muttered. I felt his servitude disconnect from me. 1,036 fairies in Shady Grove. I turned to the spectators in the auditorium. "I'm sorry you had to see that, but he compromised what we are building here. We cannot have infiltrators. I don't care if you disagree with me. That's fine. You come talk to me about it or the council, but do not go behind my back. There will be consequences."

The faces of the twenty or so who had gathered varied from fear to appreciation. When my eyes met Fordele's again, he nodded in agreement. It surprised me, but I remembered what his wife said about them looking for a safe place. Shady Grove was safer without traitors. They filed out of the room, leaving me once again with the council minus one bear, plus one wolf who had earned my trust over the past few months. I owed it to her at this point. Hopefully, this would cement our future relationship.

"Are you okay, Grace?" Nestor asked.

"No, but it had to be done. I needed to know I could do it if necessary," I mumbled. Dylan looked like he wanted to take me home away from all of this, but he didn't move from his spot standing beside me. "We have to decide on what happens to Stephanie Davis. She was banished. She used a member of this council to regain entry into the town, but she also has a child. Diego's wife and children…" My voice cracked. Dylan didn't hold back any longer. He put his arms around me. I didn't cry, but it took me a moment to compose myself.

"Grace, the shifters have all decided to pack. No matter what the species. Diego had long opposed that decision. I think that pushed him to help Stephanie return to town. Troy and I tried to assure him that it was the best for everyone, but even his wife was concerned about his attitude toward all of it. She told me that he'd grown angry and violent since the election. She wouldn't allow us to arrest him, but we should have told you instead of keeping it within the pack. I apologize for that, but it's done. It won't happen again. Don't worry about his wife and children. They are safer now that he is gone. The pack will take care of our own," Amanda said.

"Still, he was a father," I said.

"And Stephanie is a mother," Betty said. "Do we let her off because the child is Dylan's?"

"We don't know that the child is Dylan's," Nestor said.

"Dylan's or not, the point is she broke the rules. We need to vote," I sighed.

"Death," Amanda said. She was quick to that before, even quicker this time.

"No," Betty said.

"Death," Tabitha said.

Nestor looked at Tabitha in disbelief. He thought she would vote no. He buried his face in his hand and muttered, "No."

He knew his vote would force me to make the decision. It was in my hands now. The woman who potentially ruined my dreams. The woman who brought my uncle into this town to kill me resulting in my father's death. The woman I hated more than anyone on the face of this earth or below it. But she was also the woman who was the mother of a child that might belong to the man I loved more than life itself. I looked into his eyes, but I knew he wouldn't speak to influence my decision. He would support me either way.

"Grace, you can't let her slip through the cracks again," Amanda said.

"She's right. She could do more harm than good. We can raise that boy in this town without her. It would be better for him," Tabitha added.

"Grace, you vote for what you know is right," Nestor said.

"Stop. All of you," I said quietly. "I have enough voices in my head without all of you."

With that, the only clear voice in my head spoke, "*No. You will regret it,*" Levi said.

"*Will I? I hate her. You said she was manipulating all of us,*" I said.

"*No, I said Dylan was manipulating you, but I was wrong. I was jealous, and I admit to being an immature idiot from time to time. You can't kill her. At least not until we know the truth about the boy. We might need her to find his real father. We might need her for other reasons as well. She might know things about Brock. About the Otherworld. Information to help us win the fight. Say no, Grace,*" he said.

He was right. If my reasons for keeping her alive were simply because she was a mother, then it would be wrong, because I just took a father away from his children. No matter how bad he was, he was still their father. Stephanie knew things. With the right kind of persuasion, we could find out what we needed to know about the Otherworld.

"I vote no," I said. Dylan relaxed next to me.

"Grace, please, think about this," Amanda pleaded.

"Let her explain," Nestor said. "Why did you decide to keep her alive?"

"*Claim it as your idea. You need to look strong now. Use it. I don't mind,*" Levi said.

"*Feels cheap,*" I said.

"You are a trailer park queen," he said.

"I am going to jerk a knot in your tail," I said.

"Please," he replied. I shot him a look across the room. He laughed. The council looked confused. As did Dylan.

"Ignore Levi. I voted against killing her because I see the perfect opportunity to question her about the dealings of my Uncle in the Otherworld. We could force her to tell us the truth so that we can prepare for an attack on us here or even an attack on Summer. Amanda knows this, but the rest of you might not know. Lysander was building an army of the worst of us. We know now that army is indebted to Brock for services rendered here in the real world. They will follow his orders, and from what Remington gathered back when all of this started, there are a lot of them. Fairies that got out of prison sentences thanks to Lysander, and I'm sure there were more with Krykos and his partner. Stephanie might be the key to unraveling all of this. Until the time that we decide that she is not worth the information, she lives. However, she is remanded to the motel room that she is in. If the child leaves, it needs to be with Dylan or Troy. Do you all agree?" I asked. It was already decided, but I wanted them to see my point. Levi's point. Whomever's point it was.

"I understand, but the moment she steps out, do we have permission to dispatch her?" Amanda asked.

"You will call me, and I will do it. She is my responsibility," I said.

The long day started to weigh on me, and I teetered again. "Grace," Levi called out to me across the room. I turned to face Dylan whose arms enveloped me before my knees gave out.

"Something is wrong," he said.

Tabitha hovered over me. "She looks exhausted," she said. "Take her home. I'll come by and check her."

"Levi, get over here," Dylan demanded.

"I'm sorry," I muttered. Dylan handed me to Levi who without instruction blinked us back to the trailer. He quickly took me to the bedroom, laying me on the bed. "Winnie."

"Dylan is still there. He will get her," Levi said, lightly touching my face. "Is it your father's power? Are you fighting it again?"

"No. I didn't think I was. It's just been a long day. Standing out there with Nestor. I guess I'm out of shape," I said.

"Grace, you are perfect," he said. With just a small hint of power, he added, "Rest."

My eyes fluttered with the command, then I was asleep.

CHAPTER TEN

A HEATED DEBATE RAGED AS I SLOWLY BECAME AWARE OF MY surroundings.

"She said it wasn't her father's power," Levi protested.

"Perhaps Stephanie put a curse on her. It wouldn't be hard for her. Kind of like the witches," Nestor said.

"No. It's something else, but we need to keep her safe," Dylan replied.

"I'm fine," I said.

The three men in my life turned to face me. I realized then that there was one other person in the room. My doctor and friend, Tabitha Mistborne. Beside me, a crystal glowed with purple power. Dylan walked to my bedside, sitting down next to me.

"Be honest. Are you okay?" he asked.

"I feel fine. Maybe just the stress of the last couple of days or something, but I feel normal," I said. "What do you think, Tab?"

"Do you want me to talk about your health in front of all of them?" she asked.

"In this one case, I don't mind. Otherwise, Dylan is the only one that speaks for me," I said.

"Something is draining your power. We need to find the source.

It will be hard to track, but a spell or hex could definitely do it," she said.

"Maybe I should speak to my father about it," I said.

"Is he even there with you carrying around the power now?" Levi asked.

"He is," I said. "We don't know why he's still tethered to this world and my stone circle."

"What did Jenny want to talk to you about a couple of days ago?" Levi asked.

"Crap. I forgot about that," I said, bolting up out of the bed. I looked down to make sure I was still clothed, and thankfully they had left my jeans and shirt on from the previous day. I slid shoes on my feet, as I made my way to the front door.

"Where are you going?" Dylan asked.

"Hey, Momma!" Winnie said as I got to the front door.

"Hey, baby! Give me some hugs," I said as I bent down to her level. "Oh, I missed you."

"I missed you too. Are you sick again?" she asked.

"No, I'm fine. Just a bad night," I said.

"The bear man was mean. His little boy, Carlos, goes to school with me. He said his daddy was angry all the time," she said.

"Well, he's gone away for a long time now. Carlos is safe," I said.

"That's good. I will tell Mark. Mark wanted to go wolf and kill him," she said.

"Dylan!" I said.

"I heard her. Let me call Troy," he said, dialing on his cell.

"Do that and follow me," I instructed.

They all followed me down the hill to Jenny's trailer, except Nestor who stayed behind with Winnie. As we walked down the gravel road, the stench of rot got stronger.

"What the hell is that smell?" Levi asked.

"Yes, that's what she said," Dylan said talking to Troy. "I thought you should know. Yeah, man, no problem."

"I think it's that other trailer," I said pointing at the one across from Jenny's. "But this is the problem." I turned and pointed at the growing swamp behind the trailers. The sheer size had grown since I'd seen it two days ago.

"Where did that come from?" Dylan asked after hanging up the phone with Troy.

"I don't know. I meant to ask some people who lived here longer than me if they had seen it in this area before. We have had a lot of rain lately," I said. The distant sound of thunder reminded us that another storm was just over the horizon.

"Who lives in the trailer?" Tabitha asked.

"Summer ward. I dare not go through it. It would bust the whole trailer apart. Not a good first impression," I said.

Dylan marched up to the door like it was nothing, knocking on it. "Hello! Anyone home?"

As we waited for someone to answer, Jenny came out of her trailer to join us.

"It's getting closer," she said from behind me.

"I see that. Any idea what could cause it?" I asked.

"Spell. Attracted to a being, which I swear isn't me. Could be just natural, I suppose," she said.

"I've lived here forever. This is new," Tabitha said.

Standing water stretched through the forest. A greenish fog floated above the surface as if it were some unnatural soup. Opening my sight, I took several steps back. Levi grabbed me from behind.

"What is it?" he asked.

"Look at it," I said.

"What the hell is that?" he asked.

"Something is alive in it," I said.

Dylan ran off the porch of the trailer. "Where?" he asked.

I pointed toward the dark shape moving away from us. The hint of long tentacles with suction cups brushed the surface as it deftly moved through the water. Dylan burst into feathers and took flight. His raptor form darkened the cloudy sky like a low-flying airplane. He followed the being through the water, but the creature took off as if it knew it was being followed. Dylan circled above the bog looking for the creature. His call ripped the air in clear frustration. He flew back to us landing in front of us shifting to human form.

"Lost it," he said. "It's huge, whatever it is."

"Powerful, too," I said.

"Any ideas?" Tabitha asked.

"There are so many possibilities when it comes to water fairies. I wish Nestor would have seen it," I said.

"Hey, I'm not chopped liver," Jenny said.

"Just a second opinion," I replied. She smiled because she wasn't offended in the least.

"If the swamp gets any closer, I'll have to move," she said. "What about an Afanc?"

"An afanc is more crocodile beaver, not tentacled," Levi said. "The magical image of it definitely had tentacles. Maybe Scylla."

"No, I've never seen one of those outside of Greece," Jenny said. "Perhaps a tlanusi yi."

"What's that?" Levi asked.

"Ha! Stumped you," Jenny laughed.

"Cherokee giant river water leech. And no, it wasn't one of those. I've seen those before," Dylan said.

Jenny pouted. I was amused at the "name the water monster" debate. I listened and made mental notes.

"Yac u-mama," Jenny offered.

"Those stick to the Amazon," Levi said. "Beisht Kione."

"Oh, good one," Jenny said, offering him a hand for a high five. He slapped her hand. Then she dropped the bomb on him. "Saltwater only, though."

He laughed shaking his head at her.

"What about some of your kind?" I asked.

Jenny didn't high five me. "Could be," she admitted. "I haven't seen Peggy or Nelly in a while."

"Would you know if it were them?" I asked.

"Not really. We aren't on good terms," she said. "But I don't think it's a grindy."

"Why?"

"Instinct," she said.

We went on instinct concerning many things. I kept it in my mind that it could be another grindy, but we needed to keep searching. "Levi, see what else you can come up with. We need to keep an eye out to see if we can see it again."

"How did you see it this time?" Jenny asked.

"Magical sight," I said. Opening my sight, I looked at her. She didn't glow the same way as the dark creature in the swamp, but just because she didn't look that way in human form didn't mean she wouldn't change once her form shifted.

"I see. If I see it again, I'll snap a pic with my cell phone. Do you have Snapchat?"

"Chapsnap?" I asked causing them all to break out in laughter. Even Dylan snickered behind his hand like I couldn't see him. "What?"

"It's a phone app," Levi said. "Give me your phone." I handed him the phone while he downloaded the app.

"What's it do?"

"You can send pictures and videos," Levi said. "But they erase after they are watched."

"Well, what if I want to save the pictures?" I asked.

"I'll show you," Levi said.

"SnappyChap sounds stupid," I said. They all laughed again. "Shut up."

"Come on, Chap Snap," Dylan said offering me his hand. I took it.

"What is it really?" I asked.

"Snapchat," Levi said walking behind me. He and Tabitha walked up the hill while making an account for me. They were talking about email addresses. I didn't have an email that I knew about. "Don't worry. I made you an email account not too long ago."

"What is it?" I asked.

"TrailerParkQueen@fmail.com," he said.

"Fmail?" I asked.

"Yeah, it's fairy mail," he said.

"Who owns that?" I asked.

"A guy in town. He's cool. His name is Jeff. He knows everything about computers. We wanted to make you a website, but I figured I should get your permission first."

"You sure as hell better. And the answer is no," I said. "Lord have mercy. I don't need to be on Chat Snap or any website."

They laughed again at my botching the app name. Whatever. I'd never needed the internet. I didn't need it now. "Even Finley has Snapchat," Levi said.

"Finley is addicted to the internet," I said. "Free Porn."

"He likes the weird stuff," Levi said.

I stuck my fingers in my ears. "La la la la la. I don't want to know."

Levi waited until I took out my ears to say, "Like Hentai."

"What's Hentai?" I asked.

Levi handed my phone back to me. "Google is your friend," he smiled. "Tab, wanna go get something to eat at the diner?"

My face went blank with his sudden invitation. It surprised her too. "Um, yeah sure," she said.

"Don't google that," Dylan said looking over my shoulder.

"Why not?" I asked as Google was already searching. "Oh, shit!" Sometimes you should refrain from googling things.

Levi and Tabitha laughed at me again. I supposed I couldn't fuss at Finley anymore about his naivety. "Told you," Dylan muttered.

"Levi, when are you and Finley leaving?" I asked.

"Tomorrow morning," Levi called out as Tabitha got on the back of his Harley wearing his helmet. I cringed at him not wearing one, but I figured he was powerful enough to protect himself if something happened. It wasn't like it was a whole mile from here to there. Maybe a part of me hated seeing him ride off with my best friend, which was something I could never admit.

"Want to go talk to your father?" Dylan asked.

"Not right now. I'm going to go color or something with Winnie. I missed her," I said.

"Okay. I'm going to check on Devin," he said.

I watched him climb into the truck and head off to see Stephanie and his maybe son. Nestor and Winnie already had the crayons out when I came back inside. "Oh, can I color too?" I asked.

"Of course, but you have to pick a different book to color in," she said. "Here, color these unicorns."

"How fitting," I said. Nestor smiled but didn't comment. Spending time with my family meant the world to me. I felt better after coloring several pictures with Winnie. She let Bramble and Briar pick out our crayons, so the colors looked a lot like things in the Otherworld rather than the way they do here. Winnie loved it. Dylan was right. Even if we never had another child, I would love him and Winnie until the day we parted ways. Unfortunately, I knew that day would come sooner for Winnie than the rest of us. Until then, I would enjoy watching her learn and grow. She was one of the main reasons I didn't leave Shady Grove when Dylan died after my courthouse appearance. I was glad I had stayed.

CHAPTER ELEVEN

DYLAN CAME IN LATE. I WAS SITTING IN BED LOOKING AT ALL THE popular apps that I didn't know existed. I sent a snap to Levi, but he didn't respond. If he and Tabitha hit it off well enough, I knew exactly where they were. I tried not to think about it.

"Hey, how are you feeling?" he asked, taking off his shirt.

"I'm fine. How was Devin?" I asked.

"He's fine. Stephanie wears on my nerves, but I like the kid," he said.

"That's good. How is everything else in town?" I asked.

"Mable coordinated all the cantrips. We have them set up. If anything gets set off, there is a signal down at headquarters that goes off. I'll get an alert on my phone. That guy Jeff that Levi mentioned, really is a wiz at computer stuff," he said.

"Very good," I replied.

"You sure you are alright?" he pressed as he laid down next to me.

"Just missed you," I said, putting my phone away.

"Oh yeah?"

"Yes," I grinned.

"Prove it," he said.

"Gladly," I replied.

~

THE NEXT MORNING, I forced myself out of the bed. I felt sore from the night before making sure Dylan knew I truly missed him. He was already up fixing Winnie breakfast. I joined them in the kitchen, grabbing a cup of coffee.

"Morning, Momma," Winnie said. "Daddy said I don't have to go to school today."

"Oh really?" I asked.

"Yeah, there aren't many kids left in school. A couple of the teachers wanted a few days to get things arranged for future classes, plus I thought Winnie might like to see her Uncles off on their adventure," Dylan said.

"Sounds like a plan," I said. "I'm going to grab a shower."

"I'll grab you in the shower," Dylan said.

I giggled, leaving him to finish his cereal with Winnie.

Turning the water on hot, I stepped into the shower letting the warm water cascade down over me. I felt much better than yesterday. I think everyone just overreacted thinking there was something wrong with me. I dressed quickly hoping to spend a little time with Levi and Finley before they left.

"Can you get her ready?" I asked Dylan.

"Yeah, sure. You leaving now?" he asked.

"Yeah. I want to see them before they leave," I said.

"Alright. Go ahead. Take the car if you want," he said. I'd never driven his car. He'd never offered.

"You feeling okay?" I asked.

"Yes," he laughed.

"I'll walk," I said. Stepping out into the cloudy day, I hoped it wouldn't rain before I got to town. As I walked alone, the execution stayed in the front of my mind. Somewhere inside myself, I knew the day would come that I would have to execute a person or step down from my job. It was expected, but that didn't mean I liked it or wished to do it again. In fact, the servant disconnect from Diego was far more powerful than I imagined it would be considering how much we fought.

Dylan's attention to Devin bothered me, too. I hated to admit it because I knew Dylan just wanted what was best for the boy. However, if he was Dylan's child, it would be a constant reminder that Stephanie still had a connection to him, even if it wasn't through his heart.

THANKFULLY, the downpour didn't start until I stepped into the diner.

"Morning, Grace," Betty greeted me. "Breakfast?"

"No, just coffee," I said.

"You still feeling poorly?" she asked.

"No, just not hungry," I said taking a seat next to Finley. I kissed him on the cheek.

"What's that for?" he asked.

"Luck," I said.

"I don't need luck," he said.

"I just got you back," I lamented.

"You are the one sending me away," he smiled.

"You want to go," I said. Finley suggested the trip a week ago. I had the feeling there might be a fairy woman there waiting on him. Perhaps the elusive wife he mentioned when he returned. "Still, I will miss you."

"I'll come home. I promise," he said.

"Home?" I asked.

"Yes, with my family," he said, taking my hand in his. He squeezed it. "I'm proud of you, Glory. You are doing what father expected of you. I know last night was tough, but he used to tell me that for every bad day, there were twenty good ones to erase it. Enjoy your twenty good ones."

"With you and Levi leaving, I'm due forty," I said.

"I don't need Levi to go," he said.

"I need Levi to go," I replied.

"Maybe. I know this. His binge isn't as bad as you would think. He messes around with those women, but he never carries it all the way. He's nuts, but I thought you should know."

"I'd rather not talk about it," I said.

"Are you okay here with Dylan and his son?" he asked.

"You think the kid is his?" I asked.

"No, but while I'm in Summer I plan to find out whatever I can about it," he said. That was my brother. The politician. I missed him already. Part of me wanted to call the whole thing off, but I had to be the queen. I told everyone I was sending them there for the book, but I hoped to find out more about Rhiannon's plans for Brock, as well as the added bonus of whatever Stephanie was hiding.

Levi came in taking a seat beside me. He leaned in and kissed me on the cheek. "*Morning*," he said.

"Hey," I replied. He turned his body so that his leg would lean against mine. The physical touch sent tingles through my body. I forced back tears because Levi leaving might be the one thing that would break me outside of losing Dylan.

"*Don't cry. I can't handle it,*" he said.

"*Sorry,*" I replied.

"Morning, Levi. Breakfast?" Betty asked as she sat my cup of coffee down in front of me. I looked into it. Nestor must have been sharing his coffee recipe with Luther and Betty because it swirled with a glittery magic.

"Yes, load me up. Long trip ahead. Who knows when I'll get some good cooking again," Levi said.

"You won't find any better than my Luther's. Not here or under," she said.

"She's right. The food here is much better," Finley said. Betty winked at Finley who winked back. A flirt with a flirt.

We sat in silence as the guys ate. Sipping on my coffee, I watched people come and go. I was lost in thought when my cell rang.

"I'm going to the motel before we head to the church," Dylan said.

"Sure. You taking Winnie?" I asked.

"No, Nestor came by and picked her up. Where are you?" he asked.

"At the diner with Finley and Levi. Last meal," I said.

"Gotcha. See you soon. Love you," he said.

"Love you too," I replied.

"*He could skip that until we were gone,*" Levi said.

"*Don't be so hard on him, Levi. He's got a tough decision to make. No matter what happens he sees a young boy without a father. It's natural for him to want to take care of him,*" I said.

"*No. His job is to take care of you and Winnie. If he doesn't, then he is a failure. He should just bond with the kid and finish it. That way you will see,*" he said.

"*Are you trying to hurt me before you leave?*" I asked.

"*No. I just want you to see,*" he said.

"*See what?*" I asked.

"That he doesn't deserve you," Levi said. He got up breaking the touch I'd lingered in for too long. He stomped out of the diner. I paid for his and Finley's breakfast.

"He will get over it," Finley said.

"You would think, but I don't think he will, Fin," I said, getting up to follow him. I didn't want our last conversation to be an argument.

"Just let it go, Glory," Finley said.

"I can't," I said, as I trotted out the door to where Levi was getting on his Harley.

"I'll ride with you," I said before thinking. The rain had slacked off for the moment.

His shocked face met mine. He took off his helmet handing it to me. I slipped it over my head and took a deep breath before I mounted the bike putting my arms around his waist.

"*You sure?*" he asked.

"*Go before I change my mind,*" I said.

He revved the engine to life. The loud rumble drowned out all other noise. He settled into the seat, as he pushed the motorcycle back out of the parking space. He leaned into the throttle, and we took off with a loud rumble down the road toward the Baptist Church. When his fingers intertwined with mine, I lost it.

"*Fuck. Grace, don't do this,*" he said.

"*I can't help it. I'm sorry,*" I replied.

He held on tight as we flew down the abandoned road toward the church. He took a sharp right on to a dirt trail. "*Hold on,*" he said. Flying through the trail, he followed it with precision. I felt the magic move around us. I couldn't hear his voice, but I saw his lips moving to a song. Watching him instead of the trail. I finally got it. "I'm a cowboy, on a steel horse I ride, I'm wanted, dead or alive," he sang.

"*Cute,*" I said.

"*Whatever. I could give Bon Jovi a run for his money any day,*" he boasted. I looked up to see us approaching a hill.

"*Levi! No!*" I said.

"*You better hold on,*" he said. We hit the hill full speed, and I felt the bike drift out from between our legs for a moment. I held on to him out of pure fear. When we hit the ground, my heart pounded out of my chest. He whooped loudly, pumping his fist in the air. "*I know. You are going to jerk a knot in my tail, but it was awesome!*"

I just laughed. He was getting his one chance to show me what he could do on this death machine. The trail led back to the main road, but he stopped before we got there. He turned off the bike, then turning to me, he took off the helmet. He brushed the tears from my cheek.

"Sorry," he muttered, even though he didn't mean it.

"You should be," I said. "You had your fun."

"Not really. Unless you tell me you had fun, then I will admit to having fun," he said.

"You scared me," I said.

"But did you die?" he asked. I slapped him hard on the arm. He just laughed.

"No, I didn't," I said.

"Then you won't while I'm gone," he said.

"Oh, don't think I'm going to be lost without you, Dublin," I said.

"You will be. Maybe this is just what we need. A little breakup," he said with a grin.

I laughed at his nonsense because I knew he was just joking around. Maybe it was more truthful than either of us realized. "Either way, I am going to miss you," I said.

"How about a kiss for the road?" he asked.

"How about Dylan will kill you and never forgive me," I replied.

"He doesn't have to know," he said.

"You aren't a cheater, Levi," I said.

"No, but I want to be," he replied. Another truth that was meant as a joke.

"Go to summer. Find yourself a pretty fairy girl. Just not Riley," I said.

"I hope I don't see her," he muttered. "If I do, it will be to get the book back, and that's all. I swear it, Grace."

"Levi, you aren't bound to me like that. Finley said the binge isn't what I thought," I told him.

"Finley should mind his own business," he grumbled.

"So, it's true. You aren't really sleeping with them?" I asked.

"No, just messing around," he said.

"Messing around could mean a lot of things," I said.

"No gravy swapping," he clarified.

My laugh echoed through the forest, and his joined mine. "Just be careful and come home to me," I said. "Perhaps I would be jealous if some summer fairy girl caught your eye."

He laid his rough palm on my cheek. "Can I have one wish?" he asked.

"I don't grant wishes," I said.

"You can grant this one," he said.

I sighed. "Okay, what is it?"

"Let me see you," he said. "The real you."

I let my glamour fade until I sat before him as Gloriana, daughter of Oberon, queen of the Exiles. He traced one of the silver lines from my tattoo up my arm to my neck. His hand went up into my platinum hair, pushing it behind my ear. He traced over the edge of my ear with his finger feeling the slight tip to them. He grinned, but then pulled my face to his. I tensed, however, I felt him assure me without saying a word that he wouldn't cross a line. I felt like he already had. He pressed his forehead to mine.

"Levi, that's enough," I whimpered. His pull was strong. It was stronger than Malcolm Taggert's had been. Malcolm was an Unseelie incubus that once tried to ensnare me.

"If you are ever mine, I want you like this. As you should be, not as some glamour hiding your true self. This is the Grace I fell in love with," he said.

"Let me go," I muttered.

Gently, he released his hold on me, but I almost tumbled off the bike with the release of power between us. "Sorry. I got carried away," he said. "There is just one more thing."

"What is it?" I asked.

"I wrote a book for Dylan. He asked me to do it. It's sitting on the shelf in your vault. You will know it when you see it. If anything happens to Dylan, you go read that book," he instructed.

"Why do you think something will happen to him?" I asked.

"He will explain all of that, but before I left, I wanted you to know where to find the book," he said.

"I'll just go read it now," I said.

"No, you won't. There is a spell on the book. You can't read it until it's time for you to read it," he said.

"This is nonsense," I said.

"No, it isn't. Promise me that you will read it," he said.

"You are coming back to me, and nothing is going to happen to Dylan. He's risen before, and he will do it again. Can we please stop talking about this?" I begged.

"Yeah," he said slipping the helmet back on my head. I wrapped my arms around him, holding on for the last mile of the trip. His words echoed around in my head. *As you should be, not as some glamour hiding your true self.* At one time, my glamour did hide the obvious fairy queen in me. After a while, I got used to the brunette. Granted, the brown eyes I used to hide my turquoise ones had long gone since my father's power settled into me. However, I always darkened my skin with the hint of a tan along with the dark hair. I never once considered living as Gloriana, because of the evil cold that lurked within her. I had learned to control that part of me. The brunette was a part of me, too. She was the trailer park queen. She was brash and liked her clothes short and tight. Only she wasn't as much me as she used to be. It was something to think about, but not because Levi wanted me that way. As far as I was concerned, Dylan and I would be together for a very long time.

When we arrived at the church, Dylan and everyone else was there waiting for us. Several girls were waiting on Levi as he climbed off the bike. "Who are they?" I asked.

"Nobody," he grumbled.

One of the girls rushed up to him. "Levi, I'm going to miss you so much. Will you please call me when you get home?" she gushed.

"Maybe, Melissa," he said. The young woman had dark brown hair with purple highlights. She wore a country music t-shirt and cowgirl boots. I made a mental note that they were extremely cute and that it was high time I bought a new pair of boots. I knew her from around town, especially at Hot Tin when Nestor would have a live musician playing. Somewhere along the way she clearly had become infatuated with Levi. I couldn't blame her or any of the other enamored fangirls.

"No, he's going to call me, Melissa Marx," another said pushing her out of the way.

Melissa quickly shoved the other girl back. I cleared my throat, and they both stopped. "Sorry," Melissa muttered.

"I don't blame you. He's hot," I said. She nodded and giggled.

I looked at Dylan who hid his smile behind his ballcap, but not very well. Several of the women pushed forward to hug Levi when Tabitha pulled up in her car. She stepped out gazing at the spectacle. Levi made eye contact with her. Amid giggles, she pushed through the crowd, grabbed Levi by the arm, then dragged him toward the church. There was a collective sigh of disappointment by the whole group. The women drifted back to their vehicles.

"What was that?" Dylan asked. He obviously was as much amused as I was.

"Fan club. I'm a little disappointed that there wasn't any hair pulling or wrestling," I said.

"Who knew Tabitha could break it up like that?" he said.

"Don't mess with Tab," I smiled.

"Definitely. You ready for this?" he asked.

"Actually, I think I am. He said his goodbye," I said.

"He's coming back," Dylan added as we walked toward the church.

"I certainly hope so," I replied.

We stepped into the Grove to find Finley in full armor. Tabitha, Nestor, Mable, Betty, and Luther all gathered to say good-bye. Troy and Amanda were here, and Winnie immediately ran to Mark.

"Grace, he can't wear this," Finley protested Levi's jeans and button-up shirt. Finley held the lute that my father had given Levi. While he was gone, I intended to find him a new guitar. I knew a few fairy crafters around the world, and I was sure I could have something special made for him.

"What do you expect him to wear?" I asked, flicking my wrist. Levi's clothes changed to a long purple tunic with purple and gold balloon pants. He looked horrified at the ensemble.

"Grace!" he growled.

"You look ridiculous. Is this what you want, Finley?" I asked, ignoring Levi's protests.

The gathered crowd laughed. "Grace, stop torturing him," Dylan said.

I waved my hand replacing the pants with trim breeches and a long ornate tunic tied with a silver and blue belt. He looked down at it, cocking his head sideways. I walked over to him as he admired it. "I like this," he said.

"My father wore something very similar. I always thought he looked royal in it," I said, as I ran my hand down over the fine silk and velvet tunic. Within the brocade, small snowflakes blended in with the swirls on the trim and belt. "You are winter. You are mine. Don't forget that."

He put his hand over mine. "I won't make a fool of you, at least not on purpose," he said.

Finley patted him on the back. "Matthew is opening the portal. Let's get going," Finley said. "Love ya, Glory." Finley kissed me on the cheek, as Levi continued to hold my hand to his chest. Dylan walked up beside me.

"You were right," Levi said to Dylan.

"Of course, I was," Dylan replied.

"About what?" I asked.

"Tell ya later," Dylan grinned.

As if Dylan wasn't even standing there, Levi said, "I love you. I'll be back." He leaned in kissing me gently on the cheek. Dylan grunted.

"Levi!" I scolded him quietly. He winked at me, then followed Finley into the portal.

I watched it close behind them, and fear slapped me in the face. My hand found Dylan's which squeezed as I grabbed it. "He will be back," he whispered.

"I hope so," I said. "Why didn't you punch his face just now?"

"He and I came to an understanding while you slept after the meeting. There is a line, and he won't cross it," Dylan said.

"You sure about that?" I asked, knowing about our little motorcycle ride in the woods.

Dylan continued to smile. "If he tried, then good for him. He needed to get it out of his system, but here you are with me as you should be. He's gone off on an adventure that he needs to have. And I will live my life knowing that there is someone in this world that will love and protect my family should something ever happen to me."

"Don't start that," I protested. "You can't leave me."

"I don't plan on it," he said with a weak smile.

"Tell me. What's going on?" I asked.

He kissed me on the forehead. "Not here," he said, looking around to our friends and family that had arrived to send Finley and Levi off.

"Okay," I said. We spent time with the people we cared about the most. Nestor, Mable, Tabitha, Betty, Luther, Troy, and Amanda stood talking about their experiences with the summer realm and rumors about the beautiful Queen Rhiannon. Winnie and Mark played in the field between the oaks, laughing at the butterflies floating around their heads. For a moment, everything was almost perfect in Shady Grove. I had to remind myself that this was actually the Otherworld. A small piece carved out for Matthew the druid. From my understanding, it was given to him by Rhiannon herself. His new wife, Robin stood in a long red cloak staring at me. Our last meeting hadn't been pleasant, but I hoped that somewhere along the way she and I could make amends. She seemed like a very strong woman. I admired that in her. However, I also knew with fairies that not everything was as it seemed.

CHAPTER TWELVE

Troy waited for my response to his question. He looked as though he was preparing himself to bound out of my reach. I looked at Dylan who said, "It's up to you."

"If you think you can control her, then let them out of the motel. As long as you or Amanda are with them, I don't mind. As far as that goes, I think the boy can go wherever he wants. I wish that he would allow me to speak to him," I said.

"Stephanie has made it very clear that you are to stay away from Devin," Amanda said.

"Whatever. When is the wedding?" I asked changing the subject.

Amanda smiled at Troy waiting for him to answer. We sat around a table inside Hot Tin. Winnie was running up and down the stairs to Nestor's apartment with Mark. They were making a ton of racket as most kids do. I enjoyed hearing them play and pretend. I had observed Winnie pretending to be a wolf on several occasions. I knew now it was because her "bestest" friend, Mark, was a wolf. We were at a loss on how to explain that one.

"Saturday," Troy said.

"What!" I said. "In like three days?"

"Yes, it will be a small ceremony at the church. We, of course, want you guys to be there. I'd like Winnie to be the flower girl," Amanda said.

"Of course, she will love it," I replied.

"A sweet little dress is all she needs. Nothing fancy," she said.

"She has a ton of clothes. Every time her Daddy goes to town, he comes back with something new," I said, nudging Dylan.

"Spoiled rotten," Amanda teased.

"Both of them," I replied.

"Would you stand up with me, Dylan?" Troy asked.

"I'd be honored," Dylan replied. "I have a sweet little dress I can wear, too."

"It's a wonder Levi didn't kiss you goodbye. I know it's been a while for you," I said.

Troy and Amanda laughed. I heard Nestor snickering behind the bar even though his back was turned. Dylan kissed my temple. "With those lips, he could give you a run for your money," he played back.

"I knew it!" I said. "You okay with him gone? You gonna make it?" I rubbed his shoulders, pretending to be concerned.

"I'll muddle through somehow," he said.

"Nestor, can I reserve the bar for Saturday?" I asked.

"Sure," Nestor said.

"Great! Let me throw you a post-wedding party," I said. "The hanky-panky can wait a little while."

They blushed. "That's very nice, but you don't have to, Grace," Amanda said.

"If I'm butting into your plans, you just let me know. But we could use a good shindig," I said.

"Sounds great," Troy said.

I was excited to attend a wedding. It had been a very long time. However, it was a keen reminder that I had set a date for my wedding in the fall. I chose it because it was the day that Dylan and I had first been together. It seemed appropriate. Now it just seemed ridiculously far away.

"We will take Stephanie and Devin to the diner. I'll give Betty a heads-up. Then maybe out to the park or something," Troy said.

"Call me if you need anything," Dylan said.

"We got it. Mark! Come on, buddy," Troy called out to the child.

"Oh, Dad! Can't I stay and play with Winnie?" he asked.

"Let him stay. We are going back to the trailer. He can meet the brownies," I said.

"You sure?" Amanda asked.

"Yeah, it will be fine," I said. "If they get out of hand, Dylan can handle it."

"You volunteered for this, not me," Dylan protested.

"Whatever. It's fine," I assured Troy.

"Okay. You can stay. Behave yourself!" Troy instructed the boy who jumped up and down with Winnie. They were so excited to be able to play more and meet Bramble and Briar.

"Yes, sir!" Mark said enthusiastically.

The kids continued to play as I finished off my coffee. I gathered the cups for Nestor who insisted on washing them. When I looked at Dylan, he stared at me.

"What?" I asked.

"Just thinking," he said. I pulled my chair closer to him and sat down.

"About?"

"How much I love you," he said.

"Enough to get married the moment Levi and Finley return?" I asked.

"What?" he said surprised.

"I don't want to wait anymore. I don't know if you were kidding or not before we tried the protection spell, but I'm not. We should have done it before they left," I said. Nestor stopped washing dishes to listen in on the conversation. Dylan rubbed his forehead. It worried me. He kept getting this look, and I didn't know what to attribute it to. I'd never seen him worry like this. "Tell me what is wrong. Now is the time."

He looked to Nestor who did not respond to him. Nestor's facial expression did not change. Dylan was on his own. "I'm not hiding something from you to hurt you," he said.

"I'm not hurt. I'm just worried because you get this look, whatever it is. And it drives me nuts," I said.

"Come on kids, let's go upstairs and get some snacks," Nestor said corralling Winnie and Mark.

"I don't want to do this here," he mumbled.

I touched his arm, and suddenly we sat on our own couch in the trailer. He blinked a couple of times, taking in the transport. "Wow, that was smooth. I never felt it," he said.

"Dylan," I prompted.

"Yeah, I know," he sighed leaning back on the couch. He shifted so I could lean on him, but still make eye contact. "I don't even know how to start this conversation, but I'm going to give it a try."

"Want me to stay quiet while you tell it?" I offered. A small smile escaped from his otherwise rotten demeanor.

"Yes, please. I am well aware that it will be a great burden to you," he said. I poked him in the ribs. He cleared his throat preparing himself for whatever it was he had to tell me. "My mother's people believed in being able to transcend this plane of existence. They did it by various methods, but most of the time it involved some sort of hallucinogen like peyote, morning glory, even cannabis. It was probably used much like the wormwood in your absinthe. Being able to move into that other realm involves giving control of your body to the universe by partaking in the mind-altering drug. Alcohol does the same thing for me. When I drink, I dream. My dreams are about the future," he explained.

I tried to keep quiet, but he paused as if he was waiting for my reaction. "You are a seer?" I asked.

"It's not of much use because it changes. I only get bits and pieces of things. Remember the night I called you from Tuscaloosa, Jeremiah told you they had drugged my drink?" he asked.

I remembered that he had moved to Tuscaloosa for a long time with Stephanie. He even took a leave of absence from the department. This was several years ago. He called me one night, drunk and upset. He had promised that we were friends, but sort of abandoned me to follow her and be around her high-class lawyer friends. "I remember. You got drunk at a Christmas party," I said.

"That part was true. That night I dreamed about the vrykolakas coming to get you. I woke up in a crazed panic to get back to Shady Grove. I sent you to Hot Tin, only to realize that's where they were waiting on you," he said.

"You dreamed that?" I asked.

"Yeah," he said, brushing hair out of my face that wasn't there. His warm touch on my skin had become my favorite comfort in stressful times. "I have a recurring dream when I've had too much to drink, and it started not long after the incident with the vamps. You were missing for a couple of days. Jeremiah had us combing the county looking for you when we found you near your stone circle one night," I said.

"I remember. I had felt drained, so visiting the stone seemed like the best way to recharge. However, I fell asleep on the center stone," I said. "You acted strangely that night. You were still with Stephanie then."

"I was still with her, but when I came home that night, I let the frustrations of not being able to find you for two days wash away in a bottle of whiskey. The most wonderful dream of my life flashed through my brain that night. I've had the dream multiple times since then," he said.

"It's about me?" I asked.

"Yes," he said barely above a whisper.

Finding his words seemed to become harder for him at this point. He wanted to tip-toe through this, but I couldn't understand why. I waited silently as he gathered his thoughts once again. His eyes focused on something across the room. He swallowed and began to speak again.

"The dream changed, but there were some things that never changed. You and I are standing hand in hand before Matthew Rayburn in his druid cloak with a little, brown-haired girl by your side. You are wearing a long, blue dress that flows as the breeze blows around us. At the time, I had no idea who the little girl was, but I assumed she was your child because she looked so much like you," he stopped.

"Winnie," I said, astonished that he dreamed about Winnie

years before she actually became my child. She had to have been an infant when he first had the dream.

"Winnie. Our daughter. Beside me, a young man stood up with me. Dark hair and dark brooding eyes," he laughed.

"Levi," I said. "You dreamed about our wedding?"

His smile had never been wider. "Yes, I did. Plus, I now know that my best man is your bard, Levi Rearden. Our friends and family are there, but the actual attendees sometimes change. However, there is one that is always the same. A pretty woman holding a baby in a blue blanket. The woman is Tabitha Mistborne, and the baby is…" His voice cracked.

"Our son," I finished. "That's wonderful! It just means that it was meant to be. It means that Devin isn't your child!" This news excited me, but his face remained dark as he watched me. "What is wrong? Has the dream changed?"

His face winced in pain. I felt his body tremble with fear, and I'd never seen Dylan afraid of anything other than me being hurt. I put my palm on his face to reassure him that no matter what it was he could tell me.

"I haven't dreamed in months. No matter how hard I try. The dreams are all gone," he said.

"What does that mean?" I asked.

"I don't know, Grace! It means there is no wedding. We don't have a son. We don't have a future," he said in desperation.

"No, I refuse to believe that. Did it change after Stephanie had Devin? When was the last time you dreamed it?" I asked.

"Around Christmas, but it was faded," he said.

"It proves that Devin isn't your son, because he was already born while you were still having the dream about our son," I said.

"Grace, the dreams aren't absolute," Dylan tried to explain.

"I will not let you sit here and tell me that you think you are going to die because you stopped having a wedding dream!" I said finally allowing my frustration to take over. I regretted it the moment I let the words go. However, my wonderful man didn't budge. He sat waiting for it to soak in. He believed he was going to die. "I'm calling Nestor. We will get married tomorrow."

"Grace, honey. No, don't do that. This is Amanda and Troy's wedding week. We shouldn't spoil it for them," he groaned.

"No one has to know. We will go see Matthew tonight. He can marry us, and it will be done. I'm sure I have something I could wear," I said, trying to push up off the couch. He caught my arm, pulling me back down to him.

"This is why the dreams are unreliable. Grace, what if we get married tonight and I die tomorrow?" he asked.

"Stop saying that. You aren't going to die. You just ran out of dream juice!" I protested. "You can't die and leave me here. I can't do this without you. Winnie needs you. The town needs you." I fell to pieces in his arms. He held on tight as I cried, thinking about Levi and the book he told me about. Dylan must have told him about the dream.

"I'm not going anywhere on purpose. We need to just keep living our life as we have. You have always been observant even when you pretend not to notice things. I had to tell you because you were registering my frustration with it more often. Forgive me for hiding it from you. It wasn't my intention to keep it a secret," he said.

None of that bothered me. What bothered me was that this was clearly something he believed in being a truth in his life. He could dream about the future. He proved it to be true by warning me about the vrykolakas. Now the dreams had stopped. "Mike the vape guy," I said bolting up.

"What?"

"The vault. You know the magic vape shop," I said, wiping my tears. "We can go to Mike. He has liquid for everything. I bet he has something more potent than alcohol! We can try something else, even if it is just to settle both of our nerves."

He pondered it for a moment, then nodded. "I'll try," he said. "We need to get the kids from Nestor."

Instead of skipping back to the bar, Dylan wanted to walk to town with me. So, we walked, hand in hand, to the rainbow glitter vape shop. Mike was happy to see us and to meet Dylan. He promised that he had exactly what we needed. Providing a mod and the liquid, Mike wanted us to report back to him about how it worked. He seemed to take great pride in his concoctions.

Walking to the bar, Dylan assured me that it didn't matter if it worked or not. He was doing whatever it took to make sure he stayed here to keep Winnie safe and his fiancée satisfied. I laughed as if all I needed from him was sex.

"Really? Dylan. You act like all I care about is sex," I said.

"It was all you cared about at one point," he said.

"I've never been that shallow," I protested.

"Just that shallow on the outside," he said with a smile.

"Exactly," I replied.

Winnie was happy to see us when we got back. Mark jumped up and down, eager to get back to the trailer to meet Bramble and Briar. Dylan took them out to the truck to get strapped in for the half-mile ride home. Nestor waited for them to leave the bar before speaking to me. I knew from the look on his face that he had something important to say.

"Is everything okay?" he asked.

"Do you know about the dream?" I asked.

His dark eyes glittered with happiness. "Yes, I know about the dream. He's had it for a very long time," he said.

"He's not having it anymore. No dreams. They are all gone," I said.

He wrinkled his forehead. "Things are changing rapidly here. It's possible whatever cosmic force that allows him to transcend time is playing catch-up. I wouldn't worry."

"He's worried that he's going to die now and that we will never get married. So, I told him we would go tonight to Matthew's to get married. No one has to know but us. He seemed to fear that option as if it would be a catalyst to his death," I said.

"Death? He thinks he is going to die?" Nestor asked.

"Yeah," I muttered fighting back tears.

"No, Grace. My experience with seers and precognitive abilities has always been that it is a temperamental gift. It doesn't mean anything. You need to hold on to the fact that he has been having the dream of being married to you with Winnie as your daughter and a son in Tabitha's arms for years. Even Levi is in the dream. It helped him through some very dark times. Now that it's faded it worries him, but don't assume the worst," Nestor said, hugging me.

"Thanks, Ness," I said.

"Go have fun with those kids. They are a hoot," he said.

I kissed him on the cheek, then joined Dylan in the truck. I told him what I had told Nestor, and what Nestor had to say.

"He's right. That dream meant a lot to me. I'm overreacting to whatever the change is to come. There is nothing in this world that will keep me from marrying you," he said.

"As soon as Finley and Levi return," I said.

"Yes. I want them both to be there," he said. "We will do this right."

"Right, and soon," I said. He laughed at my persistence.

CHAPTER THIRTEEN

SITTING IN THE CHAIR ACROSS THE ROOM FROM HIM AND WRAPPED IN a blanket, I watched Dylan sleep. Our evening with the kids had been fun. Mark and Winnie played hide the wiener with Bramble and Briar. Rufus was delighted to have a new person to scratch his belly. Rotten dog. After Troy picked up Mark, Winnie went to bed without a protest, because she had played so hard all day she was exhausted. Dylan and I curled up in the recliner watching television. We didn't talk about the dream or the vape mod.

When it got time to go to bed, he made love to me silently and strong. We didn't speak at all, just using the time to explore the other's pleasure. He smoked on the vape with Mike's magic liquid, then quickly fell asleep. I couldn't turn my brain off. So, I climbed into the chair to watch him sleep. After a while, I could tell that his eyes moved as if he were dreaming. He made no facial expressions to indicate whether it was a good dream or not. Finally, I saw his eyes settle. They didn't move for a very long time. He rolled over on the bed reaching for me.

"Grace," he mumbled, realizing I wasn't there.

"I'm here," I said, crawling back into the bed with him. He pulled me close to him spooning his body with mine. He felt hotter than he normally did. That worried me, but I dismissed it until the next morning when I woke up in a sweat. I felt like I was in a heater. I pushed away from him gently.

"What's wrong?" His voice was groggy.

"I'm burning up. You are overheating me," I giggled.

A lazy smile crossed his face. "I do know how to get you hot," he said.

"Yes, you do," I smiled. Eagerly I waited for him to tell me about the dream, but he drifted back to sleep smiling. I hated to disturb him. I didn't know how well he had been sleeping since Stephanie arrived and our world got turned on its side. We were learning to walk sideways. It seemed the natural state of things in Shady Grove. I heard Winnie get up, then turn on the television to cartoons. Rufus stirred at our bedroom door wanting out. I kissed Dylan on the cheek, then got up to let the dog out. It was time to be a Mom. Looking back to his sleeping form, a dark thought crossed over me. Even with all the confusion with Levi in my head, there was no one I wanted like Dylan. I couldn't imagine breathing, much less living without him. He wasn't allowed to die.

"Morning, Momma," Winnie said. "I think I'll have grits for breakfast."

"Grits with cheese?" I asked opening the front door to allow Rufus out to do his business. I looked across the trailer park to see Cletus and Tater outside sorting plastic bottles again. A storm cloud gathered in the distance. So much rain.

"Of course," Winnie said with sass. I laughed at her directness and wondered if she picked that up from me. I might need to tone it down a bit or my child would end up being too much like me. For a moment, I thought about Bethany, her biological mother. Winnie rarely mentioned her other than in her prayers. She always said her mother was an angel looking down on her. Wearing the key around her neck that the troll had given her at Christmas was enough for her to daily acknowledge the woman who brought her into this world. I was glad that she would remember her mother fondly. I had mixed feelings about Bethany, but I couldn't hate her. She gave me a precious gift that brightened my days.

I hadn't shaken the heat from lying in bed with Dylan, so I turned on the ceiling fan hoping to cool off the inside of the trailer. It wouldn't be long, and I'd have to turn on the window units daily. For a split second, I wished we still lived in Dylan's house. The central air conditioning would have been perfect for the humidity that would become our daily weather. Then I remembered that Stephanie took the house, and now it seemed to sit there taunting us. The home that we could never have.

We could build our own house. I had plenty of land around where my stone circle was, and it would be great for Winnie to have a big yard to play in. I knew if I called Remington Blake that he could direct me to someone who could help with building it. I decided that I would build it as quietly as possible to give it to Dylan and Winnie as a wedding gift. A part of me cringed at living in a home that didn't have wheels, but I knew my days of running were over. The anchors that held me here were my daughter and my fiancé. My life was different now, and I needed to start living it that way.

I finished Winnie's grits, stirring in the cheese when it was hot so it would melt. "To the table, little miss," I said.

She ran over to the table, where I sat the grits in front of her with a glass of milk. I also poured two tiny cups of milk for Bramble and Briar who knew it was breakfast time and appeared out of nowhere. I gave them each a vanilla wafer, then filled Rufus' bowl up with food. He stood at the front door yipping to get back inside. He hated rain, and I was sure he knew it was coming.

"All settled?" I asked.

"This is wonderful," Bramble's shrill voice assaulted my ears. I was almost used to it, but not quite.

"Thank you, Momma," Winnie said.

"Okay. I'm going to step outside and make a phone call," I said. "Put your dishes in the sink when you finish."

"Yes, ma'am," they all replied.

I opened the front door letting Rufus inside as I stepped out on the porch. After two rings, Remy answered, "Well, hello beautiful."

Remy always had a way about him that made me at ease, even when I hated him.

"Hello to you, too," I said.

"Grace, to what do I owe the immense pleasure of speaking to you this early in the morning?" he asked.

"I have a plan, and I need your help," I said.

"Is it a secret plan?" he said playfully.

"It is," I replied.

"Is it just between you and me?" he asked.

"It is," I replied.

"I swear I won't tell Dylan you are still in love with me," he said, only half teasing.

"Remy!" I scolded him.

He laughed. I couldn't help but like him. I asked him about the girl from the other night, and he said that she was someone he met in town. She was a fairy but wasn't ready to make a commitment to me or Shady Grove just yet. However, he seemed to like her very much. Of course, according to him, she was already madly in love with him. Who wouldn't be, right?

After the talk about his new lady friend, I asked him about the property that I owned, and if I could build on it. He answered all my questions as a good lawyer should.

"So, you want me to get started on it right away?" he asked.

"Yes," I replied. "How long will it take?"

"These things take time, Grace. You can't be impatient with it," he warned.

"I know, but I'm just so excited," I said.

"It's about time you outgrew that trailer," he said.

"I know. At least how long will it take to clear a space?" I asked.

"A couple of weeks at the most. A week if the ground perks," he said. "There are permits and regulations to follow."

"Alright. Give me a call when it gets cleared. I want to show it to Dylan then, but until then it's our secret," I said.

"What's our secret?" Dylan asked behind me.

"Uh-oh," Remy said.

I looked up at Dylan. "Dylan, I must tell you now. I'm madly in love with Remy. I always have been."

"What? That Nawlin's boy doesn't know how to treat a woman. Give me that phone," he joked. I handed him the phone.

"Now listen here, Remington Blake, you stay away from my woman," he said. I heard Remy's drawl reply something causing Dylan to laugh. He handed back the phone.

"You done?" I asked him.

"Yes, then I can't wait to hear what the secret is," he said.

"Ugh. Let me go take care of this, Remy. Thank you," I said into the phone.

"Good luck. Let me know if it's still a secret. I like having a secret with you, Grace," Remy teased.

"Later, you flirt," I said.

"Later you," he said, hanging up.

I turned to face Dylan as thunder rumbled behind me. "I can't tell you. It's a surprise," I said.

He rolled his eyes because he knew I wouldn't budge. "Alright. I'll let you have a secret this one time from me," he said.

"Thanks. I promise that you won't regret it," I assured him.

He kissed me on the cheek then down on my neck. I giggled trying to get away from him.

"Git you some," Cletus yelled from across the street.

"Stupid idjit," I mumbled.

Dylan held me tight then started thrusting his hips. I could tell he was looking at those fools across the street. They started whoopin' and hollerin' so loud it could have woken up the dead. The last thing we needed in Shady Grove were zombies.

"Dylan!" I said struggling to get away from him. He was laughing so hard he couldn't breathe. I was happy to see him playful this morning. I hoped his dream was a good one.

He released me, and I bolted for the front door when I felt a sting across my ass. He had spanked me going in the door. I felt the heat rise up my neck to my cheeks. I couldn't catch my breath as we both tumbled into the living room gasping for air.

"Was Momma bad, Daddy?" Winnie asked.

"See what you started?" I said pointing at her.

"Yes, she was," Dylan said sternly.

"Dylan!" I protested.

"But she promises to be good. Right, Grace?" he said.

"No," I said.

Winnie gasped, slapping her little hands over her wide-open mouth. "She might need another spanking," she said through her hands.

"Oh, that is enough," I said, stomping off to the bedroom trying not to laugh.

Dylan followed me in there. "I'll be right back, Winnie, then we can go to town to buy a new dress for the wedding," he said, as he rushed through the bedroom door to me. He slammed it hard, making a huge show.

"Do not let our daughter be the fuel for your kink!" I said.

"You are the fuel for my kink," he said with smoldering flame blue eyes.

I laughed at him. It was this ridiculousness that made our life together perfect. He stalked over to me. "Dylan," I warned him.

"Do you want your spanking now or later?" he asked.

"I really don't like that kind of thing," I said.

"I know," he smiled. "But I like to see you squirm."

"Oh, my stars!" I exclaimed. Not being able to hold back any longer, I just asked. "Did you sleep well?"

"Yes," he said simply.

"Well?" I asked.

"It seems we are still getting married," he replied.

"Don't lie to me," I said.

"I'm not. My soul is at peace. I swear it, Grace. The dream was still there," he said.

"All of it?" I asked.

"You, me, Winnie and a baby boy," he said.

My heart pounded in my chest. "Oh my," I whimpered.

"It was beautiful. I can't wait until we do it for real," he smiled. "The location was different this time though."

"Really?" I asked.

"Where was it?" I asked.

"There was a big house with a long front porch that wrapped around the side of the house. Behind it, there was a garden and a gazebo. It was there. I've never seen that place around here. I would remember it. It was beautiful. Winnie and Mark were playing on a big fort-looking jungle gym. All our friends were there. It was better than any of the other dreams," he said as his eyes glassed over.

"Don't you cry on me," I said.

"Phoenixes don't cry," he said.

"Yeah, but Dylans do. I've seen it," I said.

"I love you, Grace," he said.

CHAPTER FOURTEEN

THE RAIN POURED AS I WAVED AT DYLAN AND WINNIE. DYLAN WAS living up to his promise to take Winnie shopping. I wanted to go to the grocery store and pick up a few things for dinner. When I got to the store, I was drenched. Not even an umbrella could stop this downpour. I considered using some magic to keep it off of me, but I decided against it. We weren't fully protected from the outside just yet. No need to start throwing magic around willy-nilly.

The cool store ignited goosebumps on my wet arms when I stepped inside. Mable waved at me from the cash registers. I pushed a buggy through the aisles, picking up the items I needed for the next few days.

I turned the corner without looking and slammed my cart into Mrs. Frist.

"Good grief, Grace," she scolded, but then remembered that our stations had changed somewhat over the last few months, and she blushed with embarrassment. Mrs. Frist had always been the widow of Shady Grove. She'd had countless husbands and lovers. She even tried to get me to loan her Levi at some point, but he wasn't interested.

"I apologize. I wasn't watching where I was going," I said.

"How are you and your family?" she asked.

"We are doing very well. Thank you for asking," I said politely. I really didn't like the woman, so I pushed my cart away from her when she spoke again.

"How do you live happily when you know Dylan has had a child with Stephanie?"

Turning to her smug look, I smiled and said, "Because I love him no matter what happens. He is mine now, and the past doesn't matter. We deal and move on."

"You are still naïve, Grace. That will bite you in the ass," she said.

"Dylan bites my ass on the regular, so I'm not worried," I said. Her anger flared in her eyes, but I narrowed my gaze at her. She flicked her aggressively hair-sprayed locks over her shoulder with a huff then pushed her cart away.

It was enough to get me riled up out of my sunny disposition. By the time I got to the checkout lane, I was brooding harder than Levi on a two-day drought.

"You gotta ignore her, Grace. She has always aimed to get under your skin," Mable said.

"I know. It's just that we've had such a good couple of days. I hate to let her ruin it," I said.

"She only ruins it if you let her. Besides, you could just turn her into ice dust like the bear," Mable said.

My eyes darkened at her mention of Diego Santiago. "That isn't something to joke about Mable," I said with disdain. I realized the Unseelie fairy in her had come out in those moments. I didn't expect to see it from her. However, I knew she had been a servant of my father at one time, and an execution was a normal thing in his court. I didn't intend to make a normal thing in Shady Grove, but her tone sent chills through me.

"Forgive me, my Queen," she muttered.

"It is forgotten," I replied in a way I'd remembered my father forgiving his servants. Her eyes flashed blue then back to brown. I looked down at the jewel in my tattoo as it radiated a deep sapphire color. Invoking my father's words had ignited the power in it somehow. I knew I still had much to learn about ruling, but it was my responsibility now. I would take it seriously.

When I pushed the cart back up at the front of the store, it seemed like the rain had decided to stop. I rushed out to the truck to load my groceries, before it started raining again. I piled everything into the back seat, then pushed the cart to the corral.

Sitting down in the truck, I felt a cold rush over me. I looked to my left at the dark figure sitting in my passenger seat. I stared at the being for a moment before he turned his eyes to me. His skin was as black as midnight, but his eyes were a flashing yellow with slits for pupils, like a feline.

"Pooka," I said. The power in my tattoo brightened. He shifted away from me before speaking.

"Forgive me, my Queen, for startling you so," his voice came out as a whisper.

"How may I help you?" I asked.

"I've come to tell you the truth," he purred. I felt the rumble of contentment as it shook the windows of the truck.

"Speak it," I said bravely.

"Of the men you've loved. There is one to die, one to live, one to expose, and one to mithe," he riddled. I wanted to ask him more, but I knew the rules of the omen. He could only tell me what he willed and nothing I asked.

"I would graciously thank you for your service, but the omen is hard to bear," I said.

"It is, but I bear it for my monarch. I hope that we do not see each other again in this life or the next," he said, fading away to a dense fog, then dissipating completely.

I shuddered at his warning and couldn't begin to think of its meaning. I truly loved very few men in this world. None more than Dylan, Levi, and Nestor. It broke my heart to think of it. Laying my head down on the steering wheel, I took deep breaths trying to maintain my composure. I closed my eyes for a moment when something tapped on my window. I looked up to see Fordele standing at my door. Opening the door slightly, he pushed it open.

"Are you alright, Hannah?" he asked. "I'm sorry. Grace."

"I'm fine. Just had a visitor that threw me off a bit. Thank you for checking," I said.

He looked back over his shoulder to Wendy his wife who was putting groceries in their Volvo. I gently pushed him out of my way pacing over to her. She knew what I wanted.

"I can't help you, Grace," she said.

"Do you tell fortunes or not?" I asked.

"I do, but it's not the same as the cat," she said.

"What cat?" Fordele asked.

I got the feeling that Fordele was always a little behind when it came to his wife. I remembered our relationship. He was sweet and caring, but not the brightest bulb in the shed.

"She had a visitor who delivered the omen," she said to him, then turned to me. "But, I cannot decipher whatever he told you. The fates won't allow it. I can look at your future, but those things I will not be able to see. In fact, until they are fulfilled, I would say that any reading I did for you would be tainted. I'd rather not, but if you require it, I will."

"No. Heavens no. I would never force you," I said, realizing that I had become a little overbearing in my fright. "I'm just a little upset. It will be okay."

"Yes, it will. Come along, Fordele," she said.

"You sure you are alright?" he asked.

I nodded, trying to smile. Jumping back in the truck, I drove over to Hot Tin. The groceries I had would keep for a few minutes so I could talk to Nestor. I barreled into the bar without thinking there would be anyone there this early in the day, but Nestor stood at the bar having a cup of coffee with Remington Blake.

"Grace, what's wrong?" Remy ran up to me, bracing me as if it looked like I was about to fall down.

"Is it that obvious?" I asked.

"Yes. Come sit down," Nestor urged. "You look pale."

"She feels warm," Remy said guiding me to a stool. Nestor reached across the bar to take my hand in his.

"You are right. She's warm to the touch. What happened, Grace? Where is Dylan?"

"He's in town with Winnie buying a dress for the wedding this weekend," I said as my voice faded.

Remy picked up his cell phone off the bar. He walked away from us as Nestor focused on me.

"Tell me," he said.

"Pooka," I muttered.

"Oh, no. What did he say, Grace?" Nestor urged.

"Tabitha is on the way," Remy said.

"I don't need a doctor," I fussed.

"I don't care. I called her for myself. I've been needing a check-up," Remy said.

I had to crack a smile at his ridiculousness, but Nestor never stopped staring at me. He waited for me to repeat the omen.

"It was a pooka, Remy," I said.

"Fuck," he said.

"What did he say?" Nestor urged.

"Of the men you've loved. There is one to die, one to live, one to expose, and one to mithe," I recited.

"Well, it's not looking good for either of us, Ness," Remy said, laughing it off in his way. I wanted to protest that I never loved him, but the truth was I ran to Shady Grove because he hurt my heart. You don't get heartbroken by a sincere feeling of friendship. Heartbreak requires affection on some level. In that case, there were more candidates than just Dylan, Levi and Nestor.

"Grace, it will be okay. Did Dylan dream?" Nestor asked.

"Yes," I gulped.

"Okay, that's good. Who do you love or have you loved?" Nestor asked.

"Dylan," I gulped, squinting my eyes to force back tears. I was sick of crying over all this bullshit. What happened to my quiet life in the trailer park when no one had a clue who I was? But then I was reminded that everyone knew me, I was the out of touch fool. "You. Levi."

"I'm chopped liver, eh?" Remy said.

"Do you want to be a part of this?" I asked.

"If it means you admitting that what we once had, ages ago, was love, then yes. It's totally worth it," he teased trying to make me smile.

"Fordele," I said in response. "My father."

Nestor nodded toward Remy, but I shook my head.

"Finley," I added.

"Well, that's more than enough," Nestor said.

"And Remy," I whispered.

He leaned in close to me. "Say it again."

"Not on your life," I said. He guffawed like a fool.

"Live, die, expose, mithe," Nestor said. "Four of us."

"Can I sign up for the mithing?" Remy asked.

"Is everything a joke to you?" I shot at him.

He rubbed his forehead. "No, Grace. I just like to make things a little lighter for you. All of this stuff is depressing. I miss crazy Grace running around mouthing off to everyone," he said.

"You want mouthing? I'll start with you," I said.

"I don't think Dylan would approve," he said with a grin.

I sighed while Nestor chuckled. "Don't encourage him," I said. "This is serious."

"There's nothing you can do, Grace. You have to live your life. Don't worry about the omen. You can't stop it or change the outcome. Omens suck like that," Nestor explained then started to wipe clean glasses with his towel. I knew the nervous habit. He was thinking about something. Tabitha walked in soaked to the core.

"Why, here's the good doctor now. Tabitha, I was just telling Grace how I needed a check-up. She suggested that I needed some mouthing. Do you provide that service?" he asked her with a wink.

Her jaw dropped open at his boldness, but then she quickly recovered. "As a matter of fact, I do, but you couldn't afford me, Remington Blake."

"I bet I could negotiate a fair price," Remy coaxed. "As long as you admit it's for sale, I can come to a payment plan that would make us both happy."

I shook my head, as she reached up to feel my forehead. "You are still sick," she said.

"I feel fine. That damn pooka spooked me," I said.

"Say that three times, Tabitha. Pooka spooked. I need to make sure your mouth is worth the price," Remy continued to flirt.

Nestor held back laughter, but not very well. I couldn't hold it back any longer. He was the king of flirts. I remembered why he and I used to have so much fun. Tabitha poked at him because he'd gotten uncomfortably close to her. "Back off, Remy," she scolded him.

Leaning into her ear he said, "I did all that to make Grace smile, but now that I've accomplished that I still would like to negotiate for the mouthing because I don't think the mithing is in my future."

"Mithing?" Tabitha asked, trying to ignore him.

"He's serious, you know?" I said to her.

"What? No, he's just flirting," she said.

"I'm a serious flirt," he said. I knew that he was. Something in Tabitha's response to Remy peaked his interest. She just hadn't caught on yet. She looked at him, then at me.

"You seem fine except for the heat. When did it start?" she asked.

"Last night in bed with Dylan," I said.

"That's what happens when you sleep with a Firebird," Remy said. "Tabitha Dawn, why don't you let me show you how a real man lights a fire."

"How the hell do you know my middle name?" she asked.

"How the hell do you expect me to do my job as the lawyer of the Queen of the Exiles if I don't know about her subjects?" he returned. I was having fun watching them. Nestor seemed to be entertained as well.

"Well, it's none of your business," she said, returning to me. "Just be careful. Okay?" Remy had thrown her off. I could have had chicken pox, and she would have said it was tuberculosis at this point.

"I can think of a lot of things that aren't my business that I would love to make my business," he said.

"Is he serious?" she asked.

"Why don't you find out?" I responded.

"Remington Blake, are you asking me out?" she said turning on him.

"Absolutely," he said without hesitation. She looked at me like I needed to give her permission. I just shrugged. She had already seemingly roped Levi into something I didn't want to know about. She might as well take a roll with Remy.

"That isn't an answer," she said. "I'm going home. You may call me if you think of a way to properly ask me out." She turned on her heels and stomped out of the bar, but at the last minute, her bravado wavered. She looked back to see what he was doing, but he had turned completely away from her to look at Nestor. I looked up at him beside me and he winked at me. I laughed. Tabitha looked confused, then bumped into Dylan who was coming in the door.

"Hey, Dylan. Bye, Dylan," she said completing her exit.

I ran to him throwing my arms around his neck. "Hey, yo, what's this?" he asked.

"Pooka," I said.

His smile faded. "He finally talked to you," he said.

"He scared the shit out of me," I protested.

"Does she feel funny to you, Dylan?" Nestor asked.

He slid his hand up my arm, and his eyes widened. "Why are you warm?"

"I don't know," I said. "Someone has cursed me. Or I'm sick. Or who knows, but it doesn't matter, because someone I love is going to die."

"I thought of another," Nestor said.

We all turned to look at him. "Jeremiah."

"I do not love Jeremiah Freyman. He betrayed me," I said.

"I did a fine job of that myself, but you still loved me," Remy said.

"What the hell?" Dylan asked.

"Grace, sit down," Nestor ordered. I plopped back down on my stool.

"The pooka said that of the men I loved one would die, one would live, one would expose, and one would mithe," I said.

"So, there is a list of men that you've loved," Dylan said putting it together. "I better be on it."

"See, he wants a piece, too," Remy said, tapping the bar. Nestor sat a glass in front of him, then pulled a bottle out from under the bar that I rarely saw. Courvoisier cognac was Remy's favorite.

"You added Remy to the list," Dylan grinned as he sat next to me.

"Maybe," I said.

"Bet I can list them all," Dylan said.

"It's not like the list is that long," I said.

"Me, of course. Remy. Nestor. Levi. Finley. Oberon. Fordele. Jeremiah," he said. "Grace, you really should open your heart more." I rolled my eyes. They all thought this was a joke.

"One of you is going to die, and you are playing a game," I pouted. Dylan put his arm around my waist, turning my face to him with his finger under my chin.

"No, Glory. We understand the repercussions, but there is nothing we can do to stop it. An omen is just a warning. It prepares you for the inevitable. It's not a tool. It's an edict. It's better to live on and just let it happen," he said.

"Oberon is eliminated by default," Remy said.

"I agree. Our chances just went up by a few percentage points," Dylan joked.

I still had a difficult time finding the humor in their game. "Where is Winnie?"

"I dropped her off at Troy and Amanda's. She's practicing dropping petals," he said with the smile only a doting father could have.

"I bet it's adorable," I said.

A car pulled up outside. We turned to see two men dressed in black with large weapons on their hips step into the bar. Dylan's hand immediately went to the concealed weapon on his back. Remy put his hand on Dylan's shoulder.

"I'm expecting a visitor," Remy said.

"Who?" I asked as the power in my tattoo flared up my arm.

Remy nodded to the door as a very well-dressed man stepped

inside. His cold blue eyes stared back at me, but his facial expression was calm. He wore a three-piece suit like I'd never seen except on television. It was dark blue with pinstripes. The shirt matched the suit with a silver tie. A large silver watch rested on his wrist. Across his shoulders sat a wool coat. One of the men removed the coat, draping it over his arm. The man's face broke into a smile as Remy stepped forward.

"Well, met, Tennyson Schuyler," Remy said clasping arms with the man who was beefy. His arms looked like the driveshaft of my pickup. They were hard, tattooed, and muscular. His perfectly tailored suit stretched when he flexed his biceps. His presence was formidable, to say the least.

"Met and well, Remington Blake. You did not tell me that there would be a welcoming party," he said, looking at me. I should say he leered, but I didn't get a good look because Dylan stepped in front of me. Tennyson found it amusing as the light of humor danced in his eyes.

"It was by pure happenstance, I assure you," Remy said. "This is Sheriff Dylan Riggs."

"I am well aware of Mr. Riggs. It is good to meet you in person," Tennyson said offering a hand to Dylan who did not accept it. "I understand, Mr. Riggs. I wouldn't shake my hand either."

Dylan didn't move. He only stared at the man.

Tennyson's smile faded. "I would like to give you all the details of that night, but I'm not cleared to do that right now. I'm sure Jeremiah told you something."

"Jeremiah told me a lot of things over the years including the two of you plotting to shoot me on purpose for show," Dylan said.

I hadn't been afraid of the imposing man until that moment. I moved closer to Dylan.

"I humbly ask for your forgiveness. We felt it was necessary to keep up appearances. As it turns out, we were right. Sergio managed to pull off his aspirations for the Otherworld, and now we need to band together to stop him," Tennyson said.

"Dylan, perhaps we could clear this up later?" Remy suggested.

Dylan didn't relax.

"I would very much like to meet her," Tennyson said.

"Dylan," I muttered.

"Grace, he's a mob boss. He's had shady dealings all over the East Coast," Dylan said through gritted teeth.

"Frankly, Son, you give me too little credit. My dealings have always been worldwide, but my focus now is Shady Grove. Remy invited me here to discuss trade. You've closed off this city from the rest of the world, but you can't possibly provide all that is needed to sustain life here. I have businesses and the capability to keep Shady Grove supplied and safe," he said.

"Dylan, we need to discuss this with him," Nestor said. Nestor always had a way of calming a situation. I felt Dylan relax, removing his hand from the butt of his gun.

"Tennyson Schuyler, I'd like you to meet the daughter of our king, Grace Ann Bryant, Queen of the Exiles," Remy said, hoping Dylan would move.

Dylan stepped sideways, clasping my hand to prevent Tennyson from doing anything other than shaking my hand. I stepped forward. Tennyson took a page out of Remy's book of flirtation.

"Grace Ann Bryant, I've heard tales of your beauty, but they pale in comparison to the truth. I'm very pleased to meet you. I hope that we can form a partnership that will be mutually beneficial," he said, kissing the back of my hand.

"Flattery is welcomed, but will not affect me in any way, Mr. Schuyler," I replied.

"Tenny. My friends call me Tenny," he said.

"Mr. Schuyler, shooting my fiancé is a bad way to start a relationship," I said.

"It happened a couple of years ago, and it was done with the full knowledge that he would return to life," he said. "I swear to you that it will not happen again. I also swear that I am here for the good of the fairies here in Shady Grove. Your father and I had many dealings over the years. I admired his rule, and he admired my business. I hope that you and I can have the same relationship."

"Remington, do you think you might have given me a warning about this?" I asked trying to remain cold and aloof.

"Yes, well, I didn't expect you to be here tonight. I've been Mr. Schuyler's lawyer for many years. Long before I ever met you. He's an honest man. His reputation might be a little dark, and his methods extreme, but the truth is harder to come by these days."

I couldn't agree more with that statement. I wondered when this shooting happened, and how Jeremiah was involved. Dylan would tell me later, so I didn't concern myself with that so much as I did a very wealthy mob boss standing in my town. Nestor seemed to be okay with him here.

"Shall we sit?" Remy asked. "Would you like Grace to join us, Tennyson?"

"I would like that very much. It is just a preliminary meeting, but I'd love to get to know her better," he said as he sat down at one of Nestor's tables. Nestor circled the end of the bar with a glass of the same liquor he had poured for Remy, placing the glass in front of Tennyson.

"Nestor Gwinn, it is good to see you again. How is Mable?" he asked.

"She is well. Thank you for asking," Nestor replied, then retreated back to his spot behind the bar. He lifted his eyebrow to ask me if I wanted a drink. I scowled in response.

Dylan pulled out a chair for me, and before my butt hit the seat, Tennyson Schuyler was no longer dealing with the trailer park queen, he was dealing with Gloriana. My glamour shifted to my true self. I wore a prim, light blue business dress with an iridescent pearl necklace. Dylan kissed me on the cheek. "Do you want me to sit, my Queen?" he whispered.

"Of course," I responded.

Tennyson approved of the change as if he knew I meant business, and he preferred it that way. He took several sips of his glass, as Remy sat down with his across from Dylan and me.

"Grace, to get you in the loop, I have these proposals from Mr. Schuyler's distribution company based in Tuscaloosa. They handle essential need items like food and clothing that can be delivered to the Food Mart as well as the other small shops in town. Also, they have provided us with a catalog to distribute to the citizens of Shady Grove. We can schedule regular drop-offs at a central location. Mr. Schuyler is also proposing the management of funds in and out of the local bank. He will not control the bank, just be in charge of the transport of human currency in and out of town. His network includes fairies and aware humans. Anyone that comes into town for his business will be screened before they are allowed to make deliveries or pick-ups. You should also know that any other goods that are needed including alcohol, tobacco and other fairy-related items are part of Mr. Schuyler's vast empire. He is perfectly set up to be able to aid us with the isolation of the town," Remy said. He handed me a folder full of proposals. A long list of goods and amenities were followed by a list of items that could be accessed by request. Remy was right. Mr. Schuyler's empire touched every facet of life. I wondered if it was a coincidence that he was set up so perfectly to help us in this situation.

"Remington, tell her everything. Leave nothing out. I have no desire to meet my end by her hand," Tennyson instructed.

Remy drew in a deep breath. "Grace, Tennyson is deeply connected with your father's family. He…"

"He's my uncle. Like Brock," I said. I knew he was the moment I shifted to my fairy form. My father's power identified him immediately.

"I assure you that I am nothing like Brockton," he said. "He is an arrogant pissant. I look forward to the day you turn him to dust."

"Me?" I questioned.

"Considering the power that he has drawn from the Otherworld since he moved there, outside of your Bard, you are the only one that can destroy him. For you, it will be a flick of the wrist. The hard part will be getting to him," he said. "I will help from this side in whatever way I can. However, I will never step foot in the Otherworld again."

"Give me one good reason I should trust you for anything," I said, leaning over the table.

"I have nothing to gain from my dealings here. I'm not marking up the prices or collecting fees as I normally would from humans. My support is offered at cost," he said.

"Forgive me if I'm not impressed," I said.

He laughed, as Remy looked nervous. "I'm a businessman, Gloriana. That is all. Fairy politics bore me. I suppose they do you as well or you would have taken out Brock by now. You seem quite content here in your little exile world. I'm just here to keep it supplied. Like it or not, my Queen, I'm on your side."

"I will look these over. May I contact you through Remy?" I asked.

"Of course. I do wish we could come to an agreement tonight," he said.

"You will not force my hand," I said.

"As shrewd as Oberon, but more beautiful. He would be proud of you," he smiled.

"He is," I said. He finally showed something other than the placid look on his face. Surprise twinged around the edges of his mouth. I narrowed my eyes at him and smiled.

"Is?" he questioned directly.

"Is."

He waved his hand over his head. The two henchmen left the bar. A storm roared outside as Tennyson Schuyler, just another one of my extended family, leaned in on the table to look me in the eye. "Does my brother live?"

"No," I replied.

"Then tell me your meaning," he said. "I wish to make amends."

"I will speak to him and get back with you," I said.

"Do it now," he ordered.

"I beg your pardon. Tennyson Schuyler, I don't care how vast your empire is, when you are in my realm you will show some respect," I growled. "Don't fucking test me." Dylan huffed next to me. It was an amused huff. Nestor's eyes twinkled in the darkness behind the bar. Even Remy seemed to like my sass. I was glad I could entertain them, but I meant it. Part of being the queen meant my subjects and visitors showed respect for who I was. I wouldn't speak to him again until he apologized.

"Gloriana, you must allow me to speak to him. It is imperative," he said.

I didn't speak. I gave him the same placid look he'd given us all night.

Remy started to speak, but Schuyler put his hand up to him. Remy clamped his mouth shut.

"You are an impertinent child," he huffed, standing from his seat. He buttoned his suit coat while staring down at me. When he grabbed the handle of the door, he pulled, but the door was frozen shut. I would get my apology.

"You are not dismissed," I said.

"Why are you holding court in a dive bar?" he asked.

"I believe that you mistake my power and authority here. It's given to me by my subjects. Those in this room. Those in this city. Those who are here in heart. Until you respect that, you may not leave," I said.

I stood to face him. The dress lengthened as if my magic knew it was time to make him see me as a queen. The tattoo flared silver filigree down my arm and across my chest. My crown with its long crystalline horn sat on my head. Pacing toward him slowly, he did not look away from me until the last moment when his eyes dropped to the floor. Even the most defiant in my father's kingdom could not look him in the eye when he got in their face. He never had to speak a word before they were cowering before him.

"You have some doubt of who I really am? Please take a long look. I've allowed far too many fairies to walk over me in the attempt to refrain from snuffing out their lives. Do you understand, Uncle Tenny?" I asked.

"Yes, my Queen," he muttered. It was still disrespectful. And that was when he made his move, his hand moved to my neck quickly wrapping his long fingers around it. He shifted to his fairy form with long black hair cascading down his back. His hand froze the moment it touched my skin. I heard Dylan's chair hit the ground and the click of a chambered bullet. I held my hand up to hold him back.

"Let her go," Dylan growled.

He could not let me go. He was stuck, looking me in the eye. I wanted him to see the power swirling around me. Suddenly he shuddered, and I knew he finally saw the darkness inside me. It made me proud in a way that I had to dig that deep to find it.

"I cannot move my hand," he said.

"If you ever move against me again, I will take everything you own and burn it to the ground. Are we clear?" I asked.

"Yes, Gloriana," he said.

"I think I deserve an apology," I said, releasing the freeze on his hand. He sank to one knee looking at the ground.

"I was mistaken, Gloriana. Forgive me for trying to order you around as if you were a child," he said.

I lifted him off the ground with my finger under his chin. "Can we be family now?" I asked.

"Yes, of course. I would like that very much," he said. I still saw defiance in his eyes, but he knew I meant what I was saying now.

"I would as well. I will look over your paperwork and meet you tomorrow evening at the community center. We will finalize any deal we make then. Is this satisfactory?" I asked.

He straightened his impeccably straight coat. "Yes. More than," he replied.

I smiled. "It has been good to meet you, Tennyson Schuyler," I said.

"And you as well, Gloriana," he said.

"Be safe in this storm, and I will see you tomorrow," I said.

He nodded, then quickly slipped out the door.

"Holy fucking shit, Grace," Remy sighed.

I pushed back the darkness that I had tapped. "Dylan," I muttered. He came to me, placing his hand on my cheek.

"Yeah?" he asked.

"I just needed a little warmth amidst the darkness," I said, looking into the depths of his warm blue eyes.

"That's why I'm here," he whispered. "You didn't do anything wrong."

"I hate that it went that far," I said. "But once he called me a child, I couldn't stand by and allow it. I can't stand by anymore."

"You are right. You have to take control of situations just like you did," he said.

"And you will pull me back?" I asked.

"Always," he said.

The thunder outside rumbled the small bar. We stood listening to it for several moments before I could take a breath that wasn't laced with evil. I leaned my forehead against Dylan's shoulder, and the warmth of his body pushed the ice queen away. I felt myself return to the trailer park girl.

Remy and Nestor spoke quietly at the bar. I hadn't even noticed they were talking. When I looked at them, they both stopped. I started to apologize, but I realized that I needed to own it. That meant not apologizing for who I was. It was under control. I was the Queen.

CHAPTER FIFTEEN

AFTER SPEAKING TO NESTOR AND REMY, IT WAS PAINFULLY OBVIOUS that if Shady Grove couldn't self-sustain, then Tennyson Schuyler was our only option. However, they agreed that he needed to be put in his place. "Any other uncles I need to know about?" I asked.

"Rossi," Remy said.

"Who is that?" I asked.

"Sergio Krykos' partner at the law firm. He was Schuyler's lawyer for a long time. He disappeared when Krykos came here for the election. No one has seen him since," Remy explained.

"Did Krykos kill him?" I asked.

"Maybe," Remy said.

"I thought of something else I need to do," I said.

"What's that?" asked Dylan.

"I need to visit Diego Santiago's wife," I said. "Pay my respects. My father always contacted the family to make sure they had everything they needed."

"Troy and Amanda checked on them earlier today," Dylan said.

"It has to be me," I said. "Royal duty."

Nestor shared a long look at Dylan. It wasn't sly at all, but Dylan nodded then finished off his coffee.

"No time like the present," he said.

As we approached the truck, it hit me. I had forgotten all about the groceries that I bought. I groaned when I opened the door to the truck. Dylan smirked, "Forget something?"

"I'm trying to be a good woman to you, mother to Winnie and a queen to this whole fucking town, but I can't seem to remember that I had a load of groceries in my vehicle," I said.

"The pooka spooked you," he said.

"Yes. Scared the shit out of me," I replied.

"Some of this is fine. The ice cream is ruined though. Aw! It's butter pecan! You don't like butter pecan!" he said.

I rolled my eyes because I had bought the ice cream for him. He kissed me on the cheek, then practically shoved me into the passenger seat. He took the ruined items and placed them in a trash bin just outside the Food Mart.

The drive out to the Santiago house didn't take long. As in most of Shady Grove, things were only a few miles apart. We pulled into the drive of the ranch farmhouse. Behind the house, a large brown barn sat with its doors open. It seemed to be dark inside. The house overlooked two large unplanted fields. "Did he not plant his crops this year?" I asked.

"It seems there has been quite a bit of trouble here at the house. He had become increasingly violent with Juanita and the kids. He was drinking a lot and never planted the fields," Dylan explained. "The community has chipped in to help them out."

"Alright. Let's do this," I said feeling more nervous about facing Juanita Santiago, than I was with Mr. Schuyler.

I tapped lightly on the door. Inside a television played cartoons as the voice of children floated around the house. As the figure that I assumed to be Juanita approached the door, I felt Dylan's warm hand on my back. She opened the door with a shocked look on her face.

"Miss Bryant. Sheriff Riggs. How may I help you?" she asked. I saw her hand tremble, and it cut through my emotions to the core. I'd killed this woman's husband. No matter how abusive he had been to her, she feared me, because she knew I could do the same to her and her children.

"I would like to sit down and talk to you for a few minutes if you have time," I said. "We can do it out here on the porch if you would like."

"Nonsense. Forgive my manners. Won't you please come in," she said.

"Julio. Maria. Upstairs. It's bath time," she called out to the kids.

Groans filled the room. It reminded me so much of Winnie. I supposed all kids hated that routine before going to bed. Two children who looked to be around nine or ten bolted past their mother, rushing up the stairs.

"Please have a seat. Can I get you something to drink?" she asked.

"No, we are fine," Dylan responded with one of his killer smiles. She seemed to lighten up with the kind tone of his voice. I decided I needed to take notes on how he handled people. It had always been well known from the moment that Dylan moved to Shady Grove that he was a kind and good man. I had never heard anyone speak an ill word of him. That's a feat in itself in the South which is full of busybodies and gossips.

"I just wanted to talk to you about Diego," I said. "It won't take long, then we will be out of your hair."

"You aren't bothering me, Miss Bryant. You are welcome in my home any time," she said.

"Thank you. That is very kind," I said, pausing to clear my throat. She sat down in a chair across from Dylan and me in their living room. She picked up a remote from the table, then clicked off the television. The table was covered with various dolls, blocks, and army men. It looked like there had been a very fashionable war. "I would like to extend my sincere condolences. I know that I was the cause of your husband's death, but I hated every moment of what happened. Is there anything I can do to help you and your family?"

She folded her hands in her lap, dropping her eyes to them. "Miss Bryant, you did me a favor that I could not have done myself.

Diego had always been rough with me, but when he started hurting the children, I didn't know what to do or where to go. I should have asked for help, but I was afraid of him. My life has been easier with him gone. I hope you do not think less of me for saying it."

"No one should have to live like that. In that case, I wish I had done it sooner. However, I try to follow the law. My offer to help stands. Even if your quality of life is better now, you are still short a member of the household. I noticed the fields aren't planted," I said.

"We will get by. We always do. Thank you though. I will let you know if we need anything," she said.

Dylan stood up, taking my hand. He knew when it was time to go. She shook my hand and Dylan's as we went out the front door. She closed it behind us with a simple, "Adios."

Walking to the car, I wondered if it was too late to plant anything. Perhaps we could all scrounge up enough help to get the field planted, then help them harvest it in the fall. There were plenty of us around, plus I knew that the gypsies back when I roamed with them enjoyed working in the fields of the nearby farmers. I could speak to Fordele and get up a crew.

"What's going through your head?" Dylan asked as we drove to pick Winnie.

"Is it too late to plant anything in those fields? I don't know anything about farming," I said.

"April and May's planting season is about the same. Peppers, tomatoes, sweet potatoes, corn, squash, cucumber, beans, and melons can all be planted now. It's not too late to make the best of it," he said.

"Well, thank you, Farmer Dylan," I said.

"Hey, I've lived here almost six years. You learn a few things along the way. You should call Deacon Giles. He's a master farmer. He could help you pick out the right thing for the fields. We could muster a crew to plant it," he said.

I smiled because I liked this part of being a queen. A ruler. Whatever the case may be. Father always said that it's the people that give you the power to rule. You have to keep them happy.

~

"Yep," I said standing at the end of the road of the trailer park.

"Yep," Jenny said.

The water from the swamp had reached the back of her house, and in the distance, we could hear an approaching storm.

"I don't get it," I said. "What the hell? Swamp out of nowhere."

"You know better than that," she said. "I'm going to pack up my things."

"No! Don't leave," I begged.

"I'll just go stay in town. Finley said I could use his apartment while he was gone," she said.

"Oh, did he?" I replied. "You miss him."

"Nah."

I lifted an eyebrow at her. Her green eyes glistened.

"Maybe a little," she said. "But I know once he finds that wife of his, I'll be out of the picture."

"I dunno. Most fairies have more than one partner," I said.

"Like you, Dylan and Levi?" she asked.

I laughed because I knew Dylan would cringe at the implication. "Dylan did kiss Levi once, but it was a spell gone awry. Other than that, Levi is not a part of our relationship."

"But he's your servant. Your bard," she said.

"I know, but beyond a kiss, before I was with Dylan, Levi and I are friends," I said. "He's probably my best friend, but yeah. Just friends." She didn't need to know about the other kiss that bound him to me permanently.

"That's a shame and a waste of a good-looking man," she said. I had to agree. Levi could make some fairy very satisfied, but I knew his heart. He would never settle. Dabble, yes. Settle, no.

"I have no idea what to do about this water. Have you seen the creature again?" I asked.

"No. The water has been quiet," she said. "Too quiet."

"I have no doubt now that it's not naturally occurring. It would help if I had control over the water stone. I'm sure it would help me," I said.

"Like the wind stone that the sylph wanted?" she asked.

"Yes," I sighed. "Maybe I just need to break down and go talk to my father."

"How is Oberon?" she asked.

"Dead," I said.

She wheezed a laugh. "So crass, Grace," she said as we stared at the rising water.

I shrugged. It was true. My father was deceased, but he still haunted me. Winnie was playing in the front yard with Dylan. I heard her squeal over my shoulder as he picked her up and threw her in the air. "He's got to get to work. I'm sorry I haven't stopped this," I said.

"Grace, one thing you will learn is you don't control everything. None of us do. It doesn't matter what gifts you have, there are just some things that are out of our control," Jenny said.

I gave her a strange look. She laughed. "I won't tell anyone how wise you are. I know you have a reputation to keep," I said.

"You do as well," she said holding up her fist to me. I bumped it, then trudged back up the hill to my trailer.

"Looks bad," Dylan said.

"Yeah, we might need to consider moving," I said.

"Who are you, and what have you done with my Grace?" he asked.

"Get to work," I said.

"There she is," he smiled kissing me on the cheek. "I'm going by the motel, then I'll be on duty. What are your plans?"

"It's time to talk to Daddy," I said. "I'll take Winnie with me."

"How are you going to explain that?" he asked.

"Who knows?" I said. "She's here now. We can't shelter her. Just protect her."

"Love you. Call me if you need me," he said jumping in the plain black cruiser.

"Love you!" I said waving to him.

"Bye, Daddy!" Winnie jumped up and down. "Where are we going?"

"To the forest," I said.

"Is Uncle Levi coming to play for the animals?" she asked. My heart skipped a beat thinking about the first time he played his guitar calling the animals of the forest. Shit.

I bent down to hug her. "Not this time, sweetheart. Climb in the truck."

As we drove out to the stone circle, I blasted the air conditioning. It had been raining for days, but today it was hotter than blue blazes. It was so hot the chickens were laying hard-boiled eggs. Winnie sang all her favorite songs. She was completely adorable all of the time. I was so blessed to have her as a part of my life. Every child needed a mother. I didn't give birth to her, but she was mine. In fact, she was more mine than any of my subjects. Except maybe Levi. My thoughts drifted to my bard and my brother. I hoped they completed their mission soon, then returned home. I'd rather Finley deal with Tennyson. He was better at the politics than I was.

When we reached the end of the 8-mile road, I was pleased to see that the forest was cut away. The land had been flattened. As a being connected to trees, I knew that trees provided us with more than just ways in and out of the Otherworld. Speaking to them, many were happy to provide goods for humans. It was a life cycle which they understood better than I could as an immortal being. The trees that stood here would have a purpose after their deaths.

"Okay, Little Miss. It's a pretty good walk from here," I said.

"Momma, what are they building?" she asked, looking at the quiet equipment. I didn't see any workers around, so I figured they were off today.

"It's a surprise," I said.

"I looooooove surprises," she said.

"Come on. I've got something to show you," I said.

She held my hand as we skipped through the forest. She twirled around, dancing and laughing the whole way. Any creature within a mile's range could probably hear her. That was one thing I'd learned about having a child, it was never quiet.

In the distance, I heard a buzzing noise. Two sparkling trails of light darted toward us. The brownies had followed us. Sneaky little buggers.

"Bramble, what do you think you are doing?" Winnie asked with her hands on her hips.

He landed on a fallen log holding his hands in front of his body as if he were innocent. "We were excited to see the King," he explained.

"We are going to see a king?" she asked looking at me.

I scowled at Bramble who eeped then ducked behind the log. Briar landed on the log, shaking her head at the cowardly pixie boy.

"He's a wimp," she said.

"The two of you should have stayed home. If you want to go with us somewhere, you should ask," I said.

"I told him that, but you know men, they never listen," Briar explained. There was some truth in there, but I figured I'd better not acknowledge it for Bramble's sake. Briar might decide to skip their playtime.

"Come on. We are almost there," I said.

"They are bad fairies," Winnie said.

"What do you mean?" I asked.

"They play with the toys and forget to clean them up unless I make them," Winnie explained. "I suppose that's not too terrible."

"No, it could be a lot worse," I said.

"Maybe Bramble could be my elf on a shelf for Christmas," she speculated.

The incarnation of a fairy doll to inspire children to behave before Christmas was laughable. At least they were depicted as mischievous creatures. If only humans knew how mischievous.

"Great Jehoshaphat!" Winnie exclaimed as we stepped into the green field with my stone circle. I laughed at her choice of expletive. At least she hadn't picked up on some of the vulgar words that came out of my mouth. Granted, I toned it down a lot when I was around her.

"This is my stone circle," I said. "It's like a big garden with stones."

"Can I run in it?" she asked.

I bent down to look at her. "Yes, you may, but before you start to play, I want you to know there is a man who I'm going to talk to at the center stone. His name is Oberon, and he is my father."

"You have a daddy?" she asked.

"Yes, just like Dylan is your father. Oberon is mine," I said.

"He's your real daddy?" she asked.

"Yes. But Winnie, you know that Dylan is your real daddy, too. There will never be anyone that loves you as much as he does," I said.

"That's because I'm wonderful," she said. At least she wasn't lying. "Daddy tells me that all the time." She flipped her hair back over her shoulder with a big grin.

"Would you like to meet my father?" I asked.

"Is he scary?" she asked.

"No, but he is a ghost," I said.

"What?" she asked.

"He's like a ghost, but he won't hurt you. He glows a pretty blue color. Want to see? I promise that I would never let anything hurt you," I said.

"Will you hold my hand?" she asked.

"Yes, of course," I said, taking her hand. We walked into the circle. As I approached the stone, it started to glow a bright blue. The field turned cooler as a breeze swept through our legs.

"Hello, my child," Oberon said as his body formed above the triquetra. "You have brought me a visitor."

"I have. Oberon, this is Winnie. My daughter," I said.

She looked at him in amazement. "His crown is awesome," she cooed.

"Winnie should have a crown, Grace. She is the daughter of a queen," he said, smiling at her. He waved his hand, and a tiny crystalline crown formed on his hand. He lowered it to her. She timidly took it from him. She looked up at me for approval.

"You can wear it," I said as she slipped it on her head.

"Oh my," she muttered. Bramble and Briar flew up next to her.

They bowed while flying then swirled around Winnie as she twirled in the grass. "Let's play!" The two pixies whooped with her, then started chasing her around the field.

I had always been wary of my father, so I double checked the crown with my sight. It had no magical residue on the crown other than its formation out of pure air.

"I'm insulted," Oberon huffed.

"Oh, please. You taught me too skeptical," I said.

"I suppose I did. She is adorable," he said. I was surprised he would admire a human child like he did, but he watched her play with the two fairies for a moment before turning back to me. "How are you, Gloriana?"

"I'm okay, but I figured it was time we talked about a few things," I said.

"As always, I'm here whether I want to be or not," he smiled.

Starting with Jeremiah, Riley and the book, I explained to him why we were trying to cut off the city from the rest of the human population. He listened as I talked about Finley and Levi going to the summer realm to retrieve the book. I told him about executing Diego Santiago, and a sadness crossed his eyes that I didn't expect to see. However, when I spoke about his brother, Tennyson Schuyler, his fair lips curled into a scowl.

"I am proud of you for putting him in his place. He is my half-brother. A fiend. He was banished from the Otherworld for a reason. I hate that you have to deal with him, but there really is no other in this country that could supply your needs. Be very wary of him," Father said.

"His reputation is dark," I said. "Of course, if I keep executing fairies, mine might match his."

"Gloriana, the bear betrayed you. It is a tough decision to extinguish a life, but it seems that his needed to be if his wife is telling the truth. Your job will never be easy, but your instincts won't forsake you. Pay attention to them. I'd like to think you got that heightened intuition from me," he said. "For example, you have not been feeling well."

"No, I haven't. I'm better today," I said.

"Your body temperature is higher than normal," he said.

"It's sweltering out here," I complained.

"It shouldn't bother you. Are you sick again?" he asked.

"I hope not. It was a mess last time, and I don't have time for it. Levi and Finley aren't here to watch my back," I said. "With Stephanie in town, I'm doing a lot of back watching."

"She is lying about the boy. Don't let Dylan fall for it," he said.

"How do you know she is lying?" I asked.

"I just know," he said.

I sighed watching Winnie lay in the grass talking to Bramble and Briar about the clouds floating by. When I met my father's eyes, one of those rare moments where he radiated love flashed before me.

"Take care of yourself, Gloriana. It seems as though you are coming into your own as a ruler. I had no doubt. Well, maybe a few doubts, but you make me proud," he said.

"Thank you, Daddy," I said. "Oh, I forgot to tell you about the swamp monster."

I explained about the water rising, the mysterious warded trailer, the monster, and Jenny.

"How is Jenny? She was always one of my favorites," he said.

"Favorite what?" I asked.

"Servant, of course. She has a set of skills that you should ask her about. When you do, tell her that I gave my blessing," he said. "As for the monster in the deep, be cautious because they are rarely what you think they are, and most of the time, they have their own human form."

"There was a pooka, too."

His face fell to a dark annoyance. "What did he say?"

"Of the men you've loved. There is one to die, one to live, one to expose, and one to mithe," I recited for my father.

He sighed deeply. "There is nothing you can do to stop the impending tragedy. However, I've learned over the years that sometimes the words don't mean what you think they do. The best thing you can do is acknowledge that you have no control of what will happen, but you can control how you respond to it. When ruling, there are surprises around every corner. No conflict is ever the same.

Remove your emotions from the equation, and like I said before, follow your instinct. I fear sad times are coming for you, Gloriana. I will be here if you need me," he said.

"Thank you, Daddy," I said. He smiled, then faded back into the power of the well.

CHAPTER SIXTEEN

Winnie and I stopped by the diner on the way home to grab lunch. We left with full bellies and milkshakes. Mine was chocolate. Hers was strawberry. We spent the afternoon talking about weddings. I supposed she had never actually been to a wedding because she had a lot of questions. Turning on the television, I pulled up the menu for movies on demand. I found one that was appropriate for her age that had a wedding. She sat mesmerized by the spectacle. It was fun to watch her. Bramble and Briar helped her practice throwing petals. She would start at the door to Levi's old room, toss petals down the short hallway, then across the living room, and into my bedroom. The brownies picked up the petals almost as soon as they hit the ground, then she would about-face, repeating the process back to Levi's door.

As she practiced, I made a call to Deacon Giles who was more than excited about helping to plant the Santiagos' fields. He promised to go over there and take a look at the soil. He said that some of the Yule Lads had been helping on his farm, so he would take them with him as well. I asked him if that was a good idea, but he assured me that he could be scarier than their mother.

Dylan called twice to check on us. He said they had run into some problems at a checkpoint with a reporter, but they were able to quickly track down the wandering fellow in the woods. The woods around Shady Grove could get you lost in an instant. Most of them were thick and covered in underbrush.

"This will surprise you," he said.

"What?" I asked.

"Robin, Matthew Rayburn's wife, applied to become a police officer," he said.

"Oh, really?"

"Yes, in fact, she's a great shot. I tested her myself," he said.

"Fantastic. I was hoping that we would be able to replace the officers that we lost when the state moved out. Have you ordered new uniforms?" I asked.

"Remy and Tennyson talked to Amanda about them. Troy and I decided that we would let her make the fashion choices," he said with a chuckle. "We wanted all black, but apparently that's too dark."

"It is. You don't want to look like the F.B.I.," I said.

"I'll be home soon. What's for dinner?" he asked.

"I haven't thought about it," I said. "I'll fix something."

"Spaghetti!" Winnie exclaimed.

"She would eat spaghetti for every meal if I let her," I said.

"Spaghetti is fine with me," Dylan said.

"Spoil her rotten, Dad," I teased him.

"Yes, I do and I will. Love ya, Grace," he said.

"Bye Darlin'," I replied as he hung up.

THAT EVENING all our cares were washed away as a storm raged outside. We sat around the table as a family, eating and laughing. Dylan and Winnie put together a princess puzzle, then he put her to bed with a story as I watched from the doorway. When he shut the door to her room, his lips found mine. The storm could have washed the trailer away. I wouldn't have noticed with the intensity of his kisses.

"What's that for?" I asked breathlessly.

"I've been thinking about it all day. I have something for you," he said

He took my hand, leading me to our bedroom. I placed bets in my head that what he had for me was in his pants. I hated to inform him that he couldn't give me something that was already mine. He turned the lights on in the bedroom, and my attention was drawn to the bed where a long white box sat with a bright blue bow.

"Dylan, what's this?" I asked.

"I can't have you jealous of Winnie. I'll spoil you both," he said.

Slipping the ribbon off the box, I opened it, then shuffled the tissue paper out of the way. Inside I found an off-white dress with lace straps and a deep v-cut neck. The fabric was light to the touch. Picking it up out of the box, I cooed with contentment. It was a beautiful dress that would reach to my knees when I wore it.

"Dylan, this is beautiful. Did you pick this out?" I asked.

"I did. I've had it for a little while waiting for the right moment to give it to you. The wedding will be a perfect time to wear it," he smiled.

I was turning into an emotional basket case because the tears flowed freely down my cheeks. He wiped them away. "Sorry," I muttered.

"Why are you crying?" he asked.

"I don't know. I love it though," I said, as I laid it back down in the box. "I should thank you properly."

"I like the sound of that," he smiled.

The storm continued its onslaught as I thanked my fiancé multiple times for his giving heart. I would have never imagined that I would have found someone so perfect for me. We had a jaded past considering our past lovers. With Stephanie, Remy, and Fordele in town, it was a constant reminder of the kind of beings we used to be, but it was also a reminder of who we had become. Who we were together.

I had never been happier in my entire life than in the moments I shared with my family.

CHAPTER SEVENTEEN

MEETING UP AT THE CHURCH FOR THE WEDDING REHEARSAL, DYLAN, Winnie and I traveled together in the truck. It was the first time we had stepped inside the church since we sent Finley and Levi into the Otherworld. They had been gone for five days which I thought was plenty of time to get to the Summer Court, acquire the book, and return safely. Things never go to plan, so I decided that they had a couple of more days before I decided to go after them.

I sat in the grass off to the side watching the procession and practice for the ceremony. Druid and pagan weddings were generally performed inside a circle of friends and family. It seemed like Troy and Amanda had made this choice. They mixed in traditional elements like the procession of the bride, but the handfasting ceremony looked to be authentic pagan. Amanda had chosen Robin Rayburn to stand up with her. When the practice ended, Amanda asked if Mark could stay with us for a few days after the wedding. She had planned on someone else keeping him, but they backed out on her at the last minute. When I told her that we would, Winnie and Mark squealed like banshees. I instantly regretted my generosity, but I knew the newlyweds would enjoy their honeymoon better without the little one.

"That was awfully nice of you," Dylan said, on the way back to the trailer.

"We might need them to return the favor," I said.

"Hopefully, Levi and Finley will be back soon," he said. "I know you miss them."

"I kept waiting for a portal to open, and both of them step out in the middle of the rehearsal," I joked.

Dylan's phone started ringing. He handed it to me because he was driving. It continued to pour down. The phone I.D. said unknown. He shrugged when I showed it to him.

"Hello?" I answered.

"Give the phone to Dylan," Stephanie ordered.

"He's driving right now, and it's storming," I said.

"Put me on speaker phone," she demanded. I clicked the speakerphone button.

"Okay," I said.

"Dylan, he is gone. I cannot find him, and the stupid cop you have at my door has the ward up. I cannot leave. You get over here right now and find our son," she growled.

"Stephanie, calm down. I'm sure he's close by. He's been cooped up in that motel room for a week," Dylan said. "I'll drop Grace and Winnie off at home and go look for him."

"Fine!" she screamed into the phone so loud I almost dropped it. The line went dead. I wanted to kill her. I had every right to kill her if I wanted to because she had returned to town after the banishment. Dylan picked up on my discontentment.

"It won't take long. He's just as tired of her as I am," he said. "I wish she would let me bring him back to the trailer with us, but she doesn't want you anywhere near him."

"Do you think he is yours now?" I asked because I was confused as to why he would want to bring a kid that wasn't his, home.

"No. Of course not. It's a trick, but he's still a kid," he said. "He needs someone to look out for him until we can find out who his father is."

I sighed because he was right, but I had opened my heart enough. It felt like I had reached my hard limit for tolerance of his ex-girlfriend and her son. Yesterday had been a wonderful day, and this one little phone call ruined my whole day. Remaining mature about the whole thing wasn't easy, but I was doing it for Dylan. However, I wasn't sure how much more I could take.

~

THE STORM SUBSIDED, but I was still up at 1 a.m. waiting to hear from Dylan. His phone was going straight to voicemail, and so I broke down. I called for help.

"Hello," a groggy voice answered.

"Troy," I said.

He perked up. "Grace, what's wrong?"

"Dylan went out after we got home to find Devin. He had run away from Stephanie for which I don't blame him. I would run away from her too, but that was hours ago. He isn't answering his phone," I said. "I know you are getting married tomorrow…"

He interrupted me, "How am I supposed to get married without my best man? Don't worry. I'll find him."

I paced the room for hours until Troy came in the front door with Dylan. He looked dazed. "What happened?" I asked.

"He was out at the old house. She was there, too. I don't know what she did to him," he said plopping Dylan down on the couch. Without willing it to happen, I shifted into the fairy queen. The temperature dropped. Winnie came out of her room to see Dylan who didn't immediately greet her as he usually did.

"Daddy, what's wrong?" she whined.

"Bramble!" I called out to the little brownie.

"Take Winnie back in her room. Play or help her get back to sleep. No magic," I said.

"As you wish, my Queen," he bowed, then prompted Winnie to go back in the room. When the door clicked shut, I touched the wall behind the couch which connected to Winnie's room. A shimmering ward wrapped around the room block out the sound from the living room.

"Go home, Troy," I said.

"Grace, I'm not leaving until he's coherent," he said.

Putting my palms on his cheeks, his eyes suddenly shot to mine. "Oh, Grace!" he huffed.

"Hey, you are fine. You are home," I said. His attention wandered. "Dylan, what happened?"

He continued to teeter back and forth. I looked at Troy who seemed more worried than I was.

"Please tell him I was sorry for this before I even did it," I said.

Before Troy could question me, I reared back, then slapped Dylan so hard on the face that my hand stung sending pain up my arm. Perhaps I should have used the non-tattooed hand.

"Fuck!" he cursed holding his cheek, but his eyes had cleared. "Did you slap me?"

"Yes," I cried. "Talk to me. What happened?"

"I can't believe you slapped me. Fuck, Grace. That hurt," he said still rubbing your cheek.

"You needed it," Troy said.

"What the hell are you doing here?" Dylan asked him.

"I brought you home, you idiot," he said.

Dylan looked back at me and groaned. "It was a trap."

"No freaking duh!" I said.

"I don't know what she wanted, but I got out of there. She's at the house with the boy. He was standing on the porch when I first saw him. You know the ward let me in, so I ran up to him, but he darted into the house. When I got there, she was right there waiting for me. The ward wouldn't let me out of the house. She thought I'd bond with the kid if we were in the house together like old times. She'd torn out all the renovations I made for us. She gutted Winnie's room," he stopped to choke on those words. From that point on, his voice was laced with venom, "She is a deranged twat, and I hate the day I ever met her. She had a spell on the boy. He was sitting in a chair the whole time watching me try to break out of my own house. He looked like Joey Blankenship the day I found her fucking him on my couch. I recall deciding that I wanted to flame through the ward. Beyond that, I don't remember anything."

"The house was in flames when Amanda and I got there. We were on foot," he said to indicate they were tracking him in wolf form. "Amanda took Stephanie and Devin back to the hotel, and I brought Dylan here. We found him passed out in the grass outside the house."

"You caught her fucking Joey on the couch, and she spelled him? Is that why he was sick back then? I thought I had done something to him," I said, backing away from him. "Why did you let her do that?"

"Troy leave," Dylan said soberly.

"Yep. Wedding tomorrow," he said nervously then ducked out the door.

"I did not let her spell Joey Blankenship," he said.

"No, but you kept her after you caught her doing that? I thought I was bad for fucking him and leaving him, but at least he did it willingly," I said.

He raised his hands out to touch me, but they trembled. "Grace, there have always been things about my relationship with her that I didn't talk about because it didn't matter anymore. We were together. You and me. I never looked back."

"Why would you stay with her?" I asked.

"I can't," he stammered.

"You can't tell me?" I screamed. "What the hell? It's not like I'm leaving. I am just trying to figure out why you still wanted to be with her after she put a spell on a helpless human!"

"Jeremiah," he muttered.

"Fucking Jeremiah. I'm going to trim his tail feathers when I see him," I fussed, pacing the room.

"Me first," Dylan grumbled, rubbing his forehead.

I stopped pacing to stare at him. What lies had he told that I didn't realize? Is that what always plagued him? Is that why he was always afraid I would leave? I loved him with every part of my being, but there were times when he lacked a backbone when it came to me. I had overlooked it, but now it was painfully clear. There were still things I did not know. His guilty eyes met mine.

"Don't worry. I'm not leaving or kicking you out. We've been through enough, but I want you to promise me that there will be a day when you hold nothing back from me. Curse, oath, or promise be damned. Promise me, Dylan," I said.

"I promise, Grace, and I hope you can forgive me," he said.

"So, the house is gone for real this time?" I asked.

"Yes," he mumbled.

"Winnie, come here," I said releasing the spell that kept her in her room. She teetered out with a blanket followed by the two little brownies. She rubbed her eyes as Dylan picked her up in his arms. He squeezed her tightly.

"I love you, Winnie," he whispered.

"I love you, too, Daddy," she said, laying her head on his shoulder.

"We are going for a ride," I said.

"Now?" he asked. "It's starting to rain again."

"I know, but it has to be now," I replied.

I grabbed my keys to the truck. He went out and strapped a sleeping Winnie in her seat. I waved goodbye to Bramble and Briar who stood in the front window with Rufus. They looked out on us as we pulled out of the trailer park in the wee hours of Saturday morning.

"I have to show you something," I said.

Driving through town as quickly as I could without putting us in danger, I found the road leading out to my stone circle. Remy had texted me earlier in the night that despite his long estimations, the lot was ready to build our new house.

"This road is going to be a mess," Dylan said.

"You always wanted to go mud riding with me," I smirked.

"Not really. After I saw how mad you were at Joey, I decided I wasn't interested in whatever that was," he said.

I sighed remembering the incident with Joey Blankenship. He was one of the few fucks I had in Shady Grove while on contract with the Sanhedrin. My tryst with him didn't go the way I wanted, and I ended up barefoot, muddy and arrested. Arrested by Dylan who hadn't been in Shady Grove very long.

Once we reached the end of the road, I flicked on the high beams as well as the light rack on the truck. It illuminated the flattened space at the end of the road.

"What happened?" he asked.

I took his warm hand in mine, and I cleared my throat. "I'm building a house," I said quietly.

"Oh, Grace," he whispered, staring out into the rainy night.

"A home for us. Winnie deserves a real house, and one day when we have a child of our own, he will have a special room, too. Don't let Stephanie ruin what we have. That boy is not yours. I hate it for him, but perhaps we can find someone else to play surrogate father for him. For her, this isn't about making you a father. It's a vendetta to destroy us and Shady Grove. This town doesn't make it without us," I said.

"Without you," he said.

"I can't live without you, so us," I said. He squeezed my hand.

"Between the birthday party and this, I'm not sure a dress measures up," he said.

"I just need you," I said.

We sat in the truck watching the rain hit the windshield. I slowly backed the truck up to turn it around. Dylan never took his eyes off the cleared place for our home. He slumped back into the seat. "Will you go by the old house?" he asked.

"You sure?"

"Yeah, I need to check something," he said.

"Okay," I replied, turning down the road that would take us to the burned ruins of his restored antebellum home.

Even through the rain, the embers smoldered where the house stood. I sighed because the house itself was a beauty. Dylan had done so much work on the house to please Winnie and me. I hurt for him as he stared at it.

"Can you see if the magic is gone?" he asked.

I switched to my fairy sight. The faint residue of the old ward was there, but it was no longer intact. Something that large was anchored by the house, and since the house was ash, so was the ward.

"Nothing there," I said.

"Be right back," he said, darting off into the rain before I could call after him.

He walked through the embers which did nothing to his skin. Small flames flared at his feet as he walked. He pushed through debris with fiery hands until he uncovered what he was trying to find. I saw him lift the old safe that used to be in the upstairs hallway, turning it to face him. He grabbed the handle with a molten hand, and the door jolted open. He shook his hand to remove the flames. His skin turned from bright amber to his normal tanned shade. He reached into the safe, dragging out an item in a plastic bag.

When he got back to the truck, he was barely wet. Just his shirt, but the rain had evaporated as it touched his skin. Carefully he opened the bag, pulling out the items inside. First, he placed the circular dish on the dashboard followed by the dainty teacup covered in red roses.

"How long have you had that?" I asked.

"Since I took it from your house," he said.

"It was broken," I muttered through tears. Yes, I was crying like a baby. Again. After he gave it to me, there was a time that I felt like he had betrayed me. Technically he had, and I still didn't understand why. In my fury, I shattered the cup and saucer on the wall of the trailer. I knew he had taken the pieces, but I never dreamed that they could be whole again.

"It's not now," he said.

My memories were flooded of the day Dylan gave me the teacup. He said I was like whiskey in a teacup. Back then I was pretty sure I was nothing but bite, but Dylan saw through all of that from very early on. He said he had always loved me. I saw that now in a pristine teacup that was once shattered.

"I'm so tired," I said.

"I'll run around. You slide over here, and I'll drive us home," he said.

I did as he asked, letting him take over. I rested the teacup in my lap as we drove. He had kept it all this time, waiting for the moment to give it back. Thankfully it survived the house disappearing and burning down. I knew then looking at the cup that Dylan and I could make it through anything together.

CHAPTER EIGHTEEN

We woke up the next afternoon to Dylan's phone buzzing. Winnie laid between us with Rufus somewhere under the sheets.

"Hello," Dylan mumbled.

I could hear Troy on the other end.

"Yeah, man. I'm fine. I'll be there in a few minutes," Dylan said. He hung up the phone as his feet thudded to the floor. I didn't look over at him. My eyes were fixed on the teacup sitting on my night-stand. "Mind if I shower?"

I rolled over to look at him. Winnie stirred as I admired him shirtless and groggy. He saw the look in my eye giving me a smirk. I knew we didn't have time for it, but I could lust. I was allowed.

"Up and at 'em, Atom Ant," I said, shaking Winnie.

"My name is not Atom Ant, Mom," she said suddenly sassy.

"Oh, my bad. Hungry?" I asked.

"Is the wedding now?" she asked in return.

"Not now, but it is today," I said. It seemed the rain had slacked up, but it still sprinkled outside. I wanted to get a good look at the bog before we left.

I fixed what basically was lunch for Winnie, but she insisted on pancakes. Thankfully, I had some of the frozen ones in the kitchen.

I fed Rufus, then provided the brownies with their morning cups of milk. Dylan took a long shower. I ached to join him, but I knew that I needed to keep an eye on Winnie. When he came out of the bedroom with only a towel around his waist, I could barely contain myself.

"Hot damn," I said.

He kissed me on the cheek. "I knew you missed Levi prancing through the house in a towel," he teased. I slapped him on the arm.

"Darlin', you make that towel look good," I said.

"Is it the wedding yet?" Winnie asked.

Dylan said, "Winnie, we have to get dressed, then we will go."

"What are you waiting on?" she asked.

"Winnie. That wasn't very nice," I said.

"Sorry, Momma," she muttered.

"No, you apologize to your Daddy," I said.

"Sorry, Daddy," she said. He kissed her on the forehead.

"I forgive you, Winnie. Grace, go get a shower," he said.

I finished off my coffee and headed toward the bathroom. "I'll fix her hair when I get out. Briar, help her get in her dress." Briar urged Winnie to finish eating, but I realized that pancakes probably weren't the best idea. "Nevermind. Kiddo. You need a bath."

"I've got it," Dylan said.

It only took an hour, but we were all dressed and ready to go. The dress that Dylan gave me was classy in a way that I didn't think fit me. I was brass and sass, but in this, I felt reserved but beautiful.

"You look amazing," he said admiring his handiwork.

"Thanks. I'm trying to see myself in it," I said.

"You are in it," he laughed.

"Fit the profile," I said.

"Not trashy enough?" he teased.

"Not even close," I laughed. "It's lovely."

He came up behind me, lifting his arms above my head. As he lowered them, his warm fingers brushed my collarbones. He slipped a necklace around my neck. A simple silver chain with a tiny teacup charm. "I bought this before we got the cup back, of course, but it's a little sassy for your lovely dress."

"It's empty," I said, staring at the tiny cup.

"There will be plenty of drinks after the wedding," he said.

I knew this to be true because I had planned the bash after the party at Hot Tin. Nestor allowed me to push the pool table out to the storage room to set up a buffet. There would be plenty to eat and drink.

Dylan loaded Winnie in the car as I walked to the bend in the road. There were close to three feet of water under Jenny's trailer. It had started to touch the underpinning of the trailer closest to hers on that side of the street. I looked at the other trailer which still glowed with the green ward.

"Yikes," Dylan said. "We need to pack our bags up. Get Winnie's stuff out of the trailer."

"Yes, we should do that tonight," I said. "Where do we go?"

"I'll ask Remy if he has anything open right now for us to use until the house is finished," he said.

"I've watched one trailer burn. I might as well watch this one flood." The clouds rumbled promising a gully washer. Just what we needed. More rain.

I found an umbrella under the seat in the truck and held it over Dylan as he got Winnie out of the truck. We rushed inside to reach the comfort of the Summer Realm hidden inside a portal in the Baptist Church. I closed the umbrella, leaning it against a tree closest to the portal. So many friends and townspeople had gathered to celebrate Troy and Amanda's big day. Dylan scooped up Winnie, rushing her off to the waiting wedding party.

As I took a place in the large circle forming around the center stone, Tabitha walked up beside me. "New look?" she asked.

"Dylan bought it for me. What do you think?" I asked.

"It's different. It looks great on you. Are you gonna get all mature on me now?" she asked.

We laughed and talked about all the people who were there when the crowd's eye was turned to the last three people to walk in the door. Tennyson Schuyler, Remington Blake and the leggy red-head who reeked of Summer.

"Who is she?" I asked.

"Rowan Flanagan. Summer Royal. Looks like she's taken up with Tennyson Schuyler," Tab said.

"My uncle," I said.

"What?" she exclaimed a little too loudly, drawing attention to us. Remy looked over at us, but instead of grinning at me like he usually did, he was smiling at Tabitha. I elbowed her in the side.

"Oof! What?"

"He's giving you the eye. Did you sleep with him?" I asked.

"Maybe," she said.

"Really?"

"Yeah," she replied, turning away from me.

"I think it's great. Despite my past with Remy, he is kind of a good guy. I just couldn't get over it," I said. "Good luck."

"You mean it?" she asked.

"Sure," I said.

"Maybe the dress is working," she teased. I elbowed her again as Matthew entered the circle. The crowd quietened down as he began to speak.

"If you mess around with Levi, I might not have the same reaction," I muttered.

"I didn't," she confessed.

"Let us all gather that we might cast the circle," he said. The crowd formed a circle around the center altar.

The crowd parted at the southern point of the circle. Troy, Dylan, and Mark entered the gathering. The circle closed behind them. They wore simple linen suits with light blue ties. They were barefoot as well.

At the northern point, Amanda, Robin, and Winnie entered the circle. Winnie threw the petals in the air instead of on the ground creating a sweet effect around the bride. Amanda's dress was simple but elegant. White chiffon with a silvery cloth belt. Robin and Winnie both wore light blue to match the men's ties. Amanda and Troy approached Matthew. As they joined hands, their love radiated from their bodies. I had known these two for several months, but I hadn't realized how joined they were. I supposed it had a lot to do with their species and the fact that Troy was an alpha male wolf.

Matthew opened a book which contained four large crystals. Each was pure quartz and the size of my hand. He walked to a stone pillar in the East.

"I call upon the spirit of air whose breath of life we share. Come now and bless this love, so be it here below as it is above," he said.

Suddenly the sylph that gave me the air stone, hovered above the pillar. She smiled at me, then nodded to the crowd. She raised her arms swirling the air around us. "Bless it here below as it is above," she said in a clear tone that echoed off the trees of the grove. She shot into the air, disappearing from sight. He laid the crystal on the pillar, and it glowed with a milky white light.

Matthew walked to the Southern pillar. "I call upon the Southern fires whose light brightens the darkness. Come now and bless this love, so be it here below as it is above."

A burst of flame flashed the gathering, then Dylan stood behind the pillar. "Bless it here below as it is above," he said with a wink to me. The crystal ignited with a glowing flame. Matthew laid it on the pillar. Dylan walked back to his spot standing beside Troy.

"I call upon the waters of the West whose flow connects us body and soul. Come now and bless this love, so be it here below as it is above."

A small pool formed at the base of the pillar, and a woman rose from it. I eagerly watched, knowing this was the woman I needed to meet in order to gain permission to use the water stone. If I had control of it, I might be able to stop the rising waters at the trailer park. The woman rose to the point where her feet almost left the water. A white dress hung from her body, drenched in the waters of the pool. Her blonde hair fell in waves down her back and across her shoulders. A golden circlet sat on her head. If she had wings, I would have thought she was an angel. Her beauty radiated around her as droplets of water fell from her entire body. On her Celtic knot embroidered belt, a long sword hung. I knew the sword. It was my father's sword. Unconsciously, I stepped toward her. Tabitha grabbed my arm, and I shook off the concentration on the weapon and the woman wearing it.

"Bless it here below as it is above," her mature voice resounded in the grove. Before sinking back into the puddle, she looked at me. A wave of sadness flowed over her face like a ripple in still water. As the top of her head disappeared into the water, Matthew took a moment to look back at me. He winked. I knew then that he was summoning the primal forces for my benefit, not just for the wedding ceremony. They didn't have to appear here, but here they were. They were here because of me.

The crystal in Matthew's hand glowed vibrant blue, and he sat it on the pillar.

Finally, he turned to the north and called the final force. "I call upon our Mother, the Earth whose gifts include life and death, love and breath. Come now and bless this love, so be it here below as it is above," he said.

A woman walked out of the circle to stand behind the pillar. I recognized her immediately. Josie, my old neighbor in the trailer park who just disappeared after I accepted the role of Queen of the Exiles, stood behind the pillar. She was either still pregnant or pregnant again. I wondered if Mother Earth was always pregnant. She wore a simple sundress that rode high in the front over her bulging belly. On her feet, she wore simple flip-flops.

"Bless it here below as it is above," she said with a smile. I watched as she waddled back to the circle of friends gathered for the ceremony. I tried to keep track of her in the crowd which wasn't huge, but she was behind a group of people. I lost sight of her quickly. At least, I knew who she was.

Matthew returned to the center and stood facing South.

The final item he pulled from the book was a braided cord. He nodded to the couple who presented their hands for a fasting. Troy held his hand palm up, while Amanda's faced palm down. She gripped his wrist as he did hers. Matthew handed the book to Robin, then laid the cord across their wrists.

"This is the tie that binds. Behold! Troy and Amanda wish to be bound by love. Each of you here are witnesses to this oath. As the cord is tied, it is not their hands that are bound, but their hearts. While the cord has two ends, their love shall be eternal. Now they will say their vows," Matthew said.

Troy spoke first. "Amanda, I am thankful for you with each passing day. Once I was a man with no pack. However, since you've come into my life, my pack has grown from one to three. I take you as my wife, and Mark as my son. I give to you my body, my heart, and my soul forever."

I saw the faint hint of tears glisten at the corners of Amanda's eyes. She took a deep breath before speaking. "Troy, I know that our relationship started off rocky, but you have been steadfast through it all. My life's course has been forever changed by you. I take you as my husband and father to my son. I give to you my body, my heart, and my soul forever."

As she finished her vows, Matthew tied the ends of the cord into a knot. He stepped back, then turned in a circle to speak to the crowd. "You are witnesses to this bond. If there is anyone here who would like to speak, the bride and groom welcome it."

I felt an urge inside of me to speak up as their Queen. Offering a blessing over their union was common practice by the Kings and Queens of the fairies. However, I didn't want to draw any attention to myself. Looking at Dylan, I waited for his eyes to meet mine. He would know my internal struggle and tell me what to do. His twinkling blue eyes met mine, then he nodded slightly. His acknowledgment encouraged me to step forward. Matthew's eyes landed on me, and he nodded.

"As the Queen of the Exiles, I am honored to attend this wedding. Thank you for your invitation and for requesting my daughter, Winnie, to be a part of your ceremony. Following the example of my father, I would like to wish you happiness and prosperity for all of your days," I said, then stepped back into the circle. I could have made a joke or quipped about marriage. However, the moment called for me to act like a royal. I tried my damnedest.

"Thank you, Gloriana," Matthew said with a slight bow.

Several other people from the town stepped up to wish them well or to tell a short story of how they came to help in their line of work. I could tell that the werewolves had made their own place in our community of misfits. Somehow the mismatched puzzle pieces of this town formed a beautiful and unique mosaic. At that moment, I was honored to be their queen.

"Your hands and hearts are bound, so shall your souls always be. Ladies and gentlemen, I pronounce them husband and wife. Troy, you may kiss your bride," Matthew smiled.

Troy didn't hesitate. He yanked their bound hands, pulling her to his body. He leaned over, planting a very unchaste kiss on her lips. I appreciated the kiss, but there were others who might find it unsettling. I had no doubt the wolves had a very healthy sex life. As I watched them, I felt his eyes on me. I met the azure flame blue of Dylan's eyes. The man knew how to smolder. It made me long for this moment for us. I had delayed it needlessly. The moment Levi and Finley returned, I wanted to be married to Dylan. Dream or no dream. It was always meant to be.

Troy and Amanda walked toward the exit portal of the grove. As they reached the circle it parted for them, but a broom filled the gap lying on the ground. They jumped it enthusiastically as the crowd cheered them on. The wedding guests filtered out of the portal, heading to the after party that I had planned at Hot Tin. Winnie ran up to me.

"Momma, wasn't that fun?" she said.

"It was. Did you like being the flower girl?" I asked.

"I did. Daddy said I could be the flower girl again when you get married," she said.

"You most certainly can," I said. "When Uncle Levi and Uncle Finley get back from their trip, then we will do it."

"Yay!" she said, jumping up and down which spilled the remaining petals out of her basket.

Dylan wrapped a warm arm around me, then kissed me on the cheek. "You want me to kiss you like that?" he asked.

"Maybe," I said.

"If you are lucky," he quipped.

"I'm feeling pretty damn lucky," I replied.

He jerked me to him, planting a hot kiss on my lips. I felt Winnie trying to wedge between us. We broke the kiss off laughing at her. "Jealous, much?" I asked her.

"What? You were embarrassing me," she said.

"Six going on sixteen," Dylan said. "Hey, Matthew said he needed to speak to you in private. I'll take her to the truck."

"Um, okay. What is it about?" I asked.

"He wouldn't tell me," he said looking worried.

"Okay. I'll be right out," I said.

Matthew and Robin waited for me at the center altar. The stones on the pillars stopped glowing once the circle was broken, but they still sat on the pillars. Robin kissed Matthew, then walked past me without looking at me, leaving me alone with the High Druid.

"Grace, thank you for your words. They were very royal," he said.

"I hoped so," I said. "What can I do for you?"

"It's not what you can do for me. It's what I can do for you," he said. I thought he meant the way he summoned the stone holders.

"Thank you for revealing those who control the stones," I said.

"It was part of the ceremony, but of course, they didn't have to show up here," he said.

"I know Josie, but I don't know the water woman," I said.

"You didn't recognize her?" he asked.

"No, but she wore my father's sword," I said.

He nodded. "She does. She gave it to him, then took it back when he died," he said. "When she is ready to meet you, she will. However, I am allowed to tell you that her name is Nimue."

"The lady of the lake," I said.

"The very one," he replied.

"Wow."

"But that isn't what I wanted to talk to you about," he said.

"Oh, really?"

"Before setting up for the wedding, I came into the grove and found this," he said holding up a silver cylinder. I knew what it was. A message from the Otherworld. He rolled it over in his hand revealing the triquetra symbol on the seal. "I assume only you can open it. I will leave you with it."

He handed me the tube, then left me alone in the grove. The warmth of summer flowed through the trees. I looked down at the cylinder, apprehensive of the contents. I clicked open the ring latch. The spell holding it closed tingled around my fingers. I knew the magic. It was from Levi.

Rushing then, I opened the tube, pulling out the parchment inside. I rolled it out revealing Levi's steady handwriting.

"Grace, we have been delayed. Things here are not what they seem. Finley is busy with his wife, and I'm anxious to get back home. However, Riley will not relinquish the book. Jeremiah was here the first day that we arrived, but I have not seen him since. I cannot express the warning that I need to with these words, but Grace, do not trust anyone. Only Dylan. The tales here in summer about your father, Brock, and Shady Grove are very different from what we have known. I'll be home as soon as I can. With all my heart, Levi."

My hands shook reading the words. They were in danger, and the danger was coming here. I felt the urge to get to Dylan as soon as possible. I rushed toward the portal when a gust of wind hit my back. Spinning around, I watched as a glowing portal opened. The cold wind came not from summer, but from my father's realm. A man tumbled through the portal, then it closed. He lifted his eyes to me. Blood covered his clothes. It ran down his face like crimson tears.

"Jeremiah?" I said, running back to him.

He held up his hand as I approached, but I ignored him, rushing to his side. He fell over in the grass before I could get to him. I rolled him over to look at his injuries. I pulled his button-up shirt apart to reveal numerous stab wounds. "You can't stop it now," he said.

"I can fix it," I said igniting the tattoo on my arm. I felt the power flowing in me greater than it ever had. Hovering over each wound, I tried to close them, but the blood continued to flow out of the rest. Jeremiah grabbed my hand, bringing it to his lips.

"Grace, I have tried to do right by you. I hope that one day you will see it that way. Please forgive me for the missteps along the way," he said. His eyes were resigned to death. I could not stop it at this point. Over the years, I had had differences with Jeremiah, but I didn't want to see him go. He brought me to Shady Grove, and now I had a family here because of it.

I brushed his hair back out of his face. It had gotten much

longer since I last saw him. He looked very much like Nestor. "No, you haven't done anything to me. You kept me safe from the Sanhedrin. You brought me here. And Dylan. And Levi. Shady Grove is here because of you."

"I followed your father's orders. There were some commands I should have fought," he said.

"What commands?" I asked.

"I took things from you that I shouldn't have," he said. "Where is Dylan?"

"He's outside with Winnie. Troy and Amanda just got married," I said.

"Stay close to him. I told him and you that I brought him here to keep you in check, but he is your greatest protector. I doubt that Levi and Finley will ever return from Summer. Things aren't what they seem," he said, choking on blood. I lifted his head to ease his pain. He was going to drown in his own blood.

"Jerry, old coot. You can't die on me. Please don't," I said, tears flowing down my face.

He reached up and brushed my cheek leaving a bloody mark. "This dress is beautiful. I'm sorry I marred it with my blood. Be the queen you were always meant to be, Grace. It will be the only thing that will save our kind."

"I'm trying, but I sure could use some help. I need you to stay," I said.

"It's too late, but I want to give back to you what I took," he said.

"What?" I asked.

"Your memories," he said, pressing his hand to my forehead.

A flash of images pulsed through my head.

Vrykolakas.

Krampus and an Ifrit.

Bottles of Absinthe Moonshine.

An exploding house.

Dylan in flames.

It overwhelmed me, and I skittered across the ground away from Jeremiah. I didn't understand any of it, but my whole perspective over the last five and a half years changed. My memories changed everything. I only thought I knew everything about my relationship with Dylan. I only knew half of it. I felt confused as the missing pieces worked their way into what I remembered.

"Why did you do this?" I asked.

He tried to answer, but only coughed up blood.

"Why?" I screamed. "You did this to us! Why?"

"I thought it was best. You were going to run," he said.

"No, I remember, Jeremiah. All I wanted to do was stay with him," I said.

He groaned rolling over on his side. "I've failed him, you and your father. I beg you to forgive me."

"Who did this to you?" I asked, jerking him by his shirt. "Who did it?"

"Your uncle. Brock," he said. "She gave me to him."

"She?"

"Rhiannon," he said. His voice faded.

"Why?" I asked. "Jeremiah! Why?"

"Appeasement," he said. "Grace, make the pain stop."

"I can't heal it," I cried.

"No, end it," he begged.

I fought anger and pain. The memories continued to flow through my head. The ones he'd taken from me. This was what Levi was trying to tell me before he left. Something about a book that he wrote for Dylan. I pushed up off the ground, looking down at Jeremiah gasping for air. The pain ate through is features.

"Grace," he muttered. "I beg you, my Queen."

"I can't hurt you. Remember," I said. "I remember that part."

"You have accepted your father's power. You own me now," he said.

The royal power of my father flowed through me like it had the day I executed Diego Santiago, but this wasn't an execution. This was mercy. I snapped my finger, and Jeremiah Freyman turned to icy dust. The warm summer air around us quickly melted the particles.

CHAPTER NINETEEN

I DARTED TO THE PORTAL, GRABBING THE UMBRELLA AT THE LAST minute. When I stepped into the parking lot, it was empty. Even Dylan was gone. I spun around in the rain looking in disbelief.

"What the hell?" I screamed into the night.

I took a deep breath, focusing on the parking lot outside the Food Mart. My body lurched through space to that point as I willed. I marched toward Hot Tin in my bloody dress. When I reached the door, I swung it open to the cacophony of noise inside. It suddenly silenced.

"Grace!" Dylan yelled from the other side of the room. I watched as he pushed through the people to get to me. "Are you hurt?" he asked running his warm hands over my body.

"It's not mine," I said.

His heart pounded as he cupped my face. "Who?"

"Jeremiah," I choked.

"What?" he asked as Troy, Amanda and Nestor came up behind him.

"Why did you leave me?" I asked.

"Matthew Rayburn said that you asked us to go ahead. He said that you would jump here," he said.

"Where is he?" I growled.

"He didn't come here," he said. "He doesn't come in the bar, remember."

His eyes searched mine. There was too much to say, and I didn't know how to start.

"I remember, Dylan," I whispered. Nestor gasped covering his mouth. I saw Betty hug Luther close just to the right of us. Deacon Giles stood against the back wall, but his tall frame stood out among the crowd. His eyes flashed as though he knew the quiet words I had spoken.

Dylan grasped my waist, lifting me off the ground. I instinctively put my legs around him, and he went back out into the rain with me. He stood me back up on the ground outside but didn't let go of my waist. Nestor followed us out the door.

"Nestor, give us a minute," he said. His voice was gruff and hollow. Nestor reluctantly stepped back into the bar.

The rain poured down on us. Our hearts pounded in unison. Using the rainwater, he brushed my cheeks wiping off the blood. He leaned into me. "Everything?" he breathed.

"Yes," I muttered. He turned me around pushing me to the wall of the bar. His mouth covered mine in a kiss so hot it made the rain sizzle on my lips. I felt my knees getting weak when he relented.

"I told you that I always loved you," he said.

"I know," I said.

"Tell me you forgive me," he said. He didn't ask, because he already knew.

"There is nothing to forgive. Jeremiah did this," I said. "He's dead now."

"Who killed him?" he asked.

"Essentially, I put him out of his misery. Brock had done a number on him. I couldn't heal all the stab wounds," I said.

"How did Brock get him?" he asked, still pressing me to the wall of Hot Tin. I felt the fire in his body. More than his normal warmth, he burned.

"Rhiannon gave him to Brock as an appeasement," I said.

"Fuck," he muttered.

"He said that Levi and Finley wouldn't come home," I choked.

"We will get them back. She gave your servant away without permission. She owes you," he said.

"No, remember. I released Jeremiah when he took the book," I said.

"You haven't released Levi or your brother. She won't cross that line," he said.

"If she does, she will think my uncle is a great guy compared to me," I said.

The rain pattered the ground around us, but we ignored it. The low rumble of a receding storm sounded from the east. He leaned his forehead against mine. "Greece?" he asked, questioning my memories.

"Vrykolakas," I said. "Deacon and Luther."

He swallowed. "The moonshine basement?"

"I just wanted the truth, but then it was taken from me," I said.

Twice he had told me who and what he was, and twice Jeremiah had taken the truth from me. Because he thought it was the right thing to do. Because he was an idiot. I remembered the letter Matthew had given me. Thinking back over it, I was skeptical of it, but only until I recalled the tingle of Levi's magic sealing the letter. I reached down into my bra and pulled out the wet note. Dylan watched me curiously.

"Matthew gave me this. It was sealed with magic. I know it's real," I said.

He opened the parchment. His eyes darted over the words. "This is bad," he said.

"There is something else that I need to tell you," I said.

"What?" he asked.

Cutting off my answer, Amanda flew out of the bar in a frenzy. We turned to her. She screamed at the top of her lungs, "Mark! Mark!" She sniffed the air, as Troy came running out the door.

"Mark!" he screamed.

"What's going on?" Dylan asked.

"Where is Winnie?" Amanda asked.

"She's inside," Dylan said.

"No, she isn't. They are both gone!" Troy said.

"Shit. Find them!" I yelled.

Troy exploded into a ball of fangs and fur. Amanda followed his lead. They howled into the raining night, then took off running toward the trailer park. Dylan and I ran behind them. My dress ripped as I hit my stride, keeping up with Dylan's long legs.

As the wolves ran past, my trailer and down the hill, I knew where the children had gone. Bramble flew up to me through the rain. "I tried to stop them, my Queen, but she wouldn't listen," he said.

"Get away from me," I scowled at him. He darted away toward my trailer. Dylan continued to run down the hill. The water was high around the last two trailers in the park. When I reached the edge of the water, I watched as Troy and Amanda scratched at the door of the weird trailer. Dylan rushed up behind them. He started to pound on the door.

"Winnie! Mark!" he screamed. When I hit the water, at full speed, it splashed up around me. He swiveled to me. "No, Grace! Stay over there. You can't get through this ward. We are going in," he said, as Troy returned to human form, standing naked in the rain. Dylan jerked off the jacket to his suit, holding it out to Amanda who had returned to human form, too. I watched as Troy ordered her to walk back to me. She protested, but he invoked his alpha status forcing her to walk away. She stomped back up to me where I still stood knee-deep in the water. I opened my sight but didn't see the creature in the water. Looking over to Jenny's trailer, I saw that the water had already made its way inside her home.

Dylan and Troy counted as they both kicked the door at the same time. It swung back on its hinges dented from the force of the werewolf and the Phoenix. They ran into the trailer without looking. Time passed by slowly, but what felt like an hour was only a few minutes. Nestor and other people from the town ran up behind us, staring at the dark trailer. It started to glow an eerie green color.

"Fuck this," I said. Before I could march toward the trailer, Nestor grabbed my arm.

"Grace, just wait. You don't know what's in there," he said. "If something happened to her..."

His voice trailed off. Flashes of a mangled Cody Martin filled my head. "Winnie!" I screamed. "Dylan!" Amanda whimpered beside me.

A small form in a blue dress appeared at the door of the trailer. "Winnie!" Nestor called out to her when my voice failed me.

"Come here, baby," I said. She stepped down into the water, and I ran toward her. She met me halfway, and I scooped her up in my arms. "What were you thinking?"

"Mark and I were pretending to be wolves. We were investigating the strange trailer," she said, as I carried her back to Nestor who hugged us both.

"Troy," Amanda muttered. I turned around to see Mark hanging on to Troy's naked body. He sprinted down the steps into the water.

"Run!" he screamed. "Run, Grace, Run!"

"Dylan!" I screamed. Nestor took Winnie from me, then ran up the hill with the other people in town. Amanda turned with Troy as he passed me. His voice sounded muffled to me, but I ignored him. My fiancé was in that trailer, and I wasn't going to leave him. Taking one step toward the trailer, I heard Nestor screaming my name, then an explosion of green flames threw me back into the water. Strong, dark arms pulled me out of the water.

Coughing up water, I strained to scream, "Dylan!"

The carcass of the trailer was engulfed in flames. It didn't matter. Dylan would rise if he died. Everything would be fine. Luther dragged me out of the water, up the hill.

"Come on, Grace," his voice sounded gruff.

"No, I am waiting on him. He will rise," I protested. "What happened in there?"

Troy's eyes were filled with fear. "She is in there," he said. "He..." He shook his head.

"Dylan!" I screamed to run back toward the trailer. Luther wrenched me back. "Dylan!"

The earth beneath us shook. My eyes met hers as she stood

amid the green flames of the trailer. Robin Rayburn stood in the middle of the trailer with a mason jar in her hand. She wore that red cloak. It flowed around her in the wind and rain. She laughed at me, as I struggled against the strong arms of Luther.

"Where is he?" I screamed.

She tucked several jars into her basket, lifting her hood over her head. She skipped across the surface of the water. Her voice echoed through the night as she moved the opposite direction deeper into the swamp.

"The big bad wolf doesn't scare me. I'm little red Robin hood," she laughed. "To grandmother's house, I go."

The earth shook again, and against the dark sky, I saw the tops of trees dropping into the abyss across the bog. Luther growled, hefting me up. I kicked and screamed as he carried me like a sack of taters. "Let me go. I have to get to him," I said. "He will rise." I got away from him for a moment.

The ground rumbled as the trees continued to fall. Cletus and Tater ran up to us holding big spotlights. They shined them down the hill. We watched as the earth opened up swallowing Jenny's trailer, the flaming green trailer, and two others before the rumbling stopped.

"No!" I screamed clutching my stomach. I dropped to my knees in pain.

"Get this place evacuated," Nestor said taking control. "Everybody out. Amanda get the kids back to Hot Tin."

Betty's soft voice broke through my screaming. "Grace. Grace. Come on, honey. We can't do anything about that right now. We gotta get out of here before it takes the rest of it."

The ground rumbled again. Another trailer sank into the depths of the unseen sinkhole.

"Now Grace! Let's go!" Nestor ordered. He grabbed my shoulders. "Let him go."

"I just got him back," I cried. "I just got him back."

"He was, is and will always be with you," Nestor said. "But Gracie, we have to go."

I nodded as the ground shook again. Turning my back on the

growing sinkhole, I walked up the hill in a daze. Walking past my trailer, I heard the whine of my little dachshund.

"Rufus," I said, running toward the trailer before they could stop me. I ran up the steps of the trailer, forcing the door open. "Rufus! Come here, boy! Bramble! Briar!" I couldn't hear the dog anymore. The earth shook the whole trailer. I teetered toward the bedroom. The trailer shimmed. I heard Nestor screaming my name outside.

I grumbled as I got down on my hands and knees to look under the bed. He liked to hide down there sometimes. "Rufus. Come on, buddy. We gotta go!" I called out to him. The trailer tilted toward the growing sinkhole. I hit my knees. In the mirror across the room, I saw myself. Dark brown locks, brown eyes, muddy and bloody dress. Brown eyes. My tattoo was red and black. Brown eyes. I took a deep breath trying to draw power enough to get out of the trailer. I couldn't look for Rufus anymore.

Nothing.

No magic.

I opened my sight but couldn't see anything except for what my normal eyes could see. As I looked around the room, the trailer lurched again. The door to the bedroom slammed. On the back side of the door, a sigil was drawn in blood. A magic dampener.

"Shit," I said trying to get to my feet. The world swirled around me. Bile crept up my throat as nausea took over. Heaving up the contents of my stomach, I hit my knees again. More water surrounded me. I poured sweat and hurled again. I continued to throw up until I dry heaved. I dragged myself to the door of the bedroom, yanking on the handle to open it. When I got it open, I tried to crawl through on my knees.

My body was shutting down on me. The last few days were taking their toll on me. The trailer tilted on its side, and I slid downward smashing into the mirror on the wall which was now the ground of the trailer. I felt the warmth of my blood, flowing out of cuts on my body from the shards of glass.

Warm blood. My blood should have been cold.

"Oh, Dylan, I'm so sorry," I cried. "Dylan."

I felt like I was falling, and for a moment, I was weightless until the trailer hit the bottom of the sinkhole. It began to fill with water. My will had surrendered to the coming deep. I couldn't fight anymore. I clutched the tiny teacup around my neck and cried. Holding my breath, the water rushed in on me now, covering me completely. I pushed upward hoping I could find a pocket of air. Finding one in the corner, I gasped for air knowing that the pocket was closing quickly as the trailer sank.

"Help," I muttered. "Help me." I knew no one could hear me.

One last inhale, and I fell into the darkness of the waters.

CHAPTER TWENTY

OVER THE YEARS, I'D HEARD TALES OF THE DARKNESS OF WATER. How its depths could rob you of your soul. The creatures of the waters were some of the nastiest of Unseelie. They could woo you, then rip out your heart, feasting on it before your eyes. I knew at any moment, that creature would show up to claim me. My lungs burned as I held the last seconds of my breath before giving into the deep. The water around me shifted suddenly. The monster had come.

The tingle of touch snaked down my right arm stopping at my wrist. I couldn't see anything in the depths, but I jerked away from it. My lungs couldn't hold anymore, and I sucked in water. Drowning sucked. I hoped the creature would kill me before the water suffocated me.

It's tentacle wrapped around my waist, pulling me toward it. The sensation of fingers digging into my side confused me. Fingers. Hands. Arms.

Someone was here.

I felt a forehead against mine. Dylan. Dylan was here.

"*Grace,*" Levi's voice echoed in my head.

Not Dylan. "*Levi, I'm dying,*" I panicked.

"I can't jump us out. There must be a spell. I have no magic," he said.

The creaking and groans of the trailer filled our heads. It split in two. Lights from above illuminated the water. Levi pushed upward dragging me with him. When we reached the surface, I tried to gasp, but my airways were full of water. Levi pounded on my back, as I coughed up water. None of the breaths I took in were all air. They were laced with the water still in my throat.

"Come on," Levi said. "Breathe, Grace. Keep breathing."

His grip was steady, as he moved us toward a tree floating in the water. I grabbed on to it. "Dylan," I said.

"I'll come back for him," he said. "We have to get you out of this water."

"No, he's dead," I said. "Jeremiah is dead."

"What the hell?" he asked.

"This is hell," I said. Searching for a way out of the sinkhole, he looked frantically around us. "Tree. Use the tree."

"It will take us into the Otherworld. What if Brock catches us?" he said.

"Then, he will kill us," I said. "But if that beast is here, we've got better chances with Brock."

The power stored in my tattoo was long gone, but I hoped that Levi had enough to open the way into the Otherworld. The other variable was that the oak that we were touching had been ripped from the ground. I couldn't guarantee that it was still connected to the Otherworld. I'd never tried using a way of a tree floating in a sinkhole. Believe it or not, this was a first for me.

"When we go through, you stay close to me," Levi said.

"I'm not sure I can walk, Levi," I said honestly. "I threw up before the trailer went down. I don't have a lot of strength."

"I'll carry you," he said. "Let's go."

Holding on to my waist, he touched the tree. I felt the power move, opening the way. Less than a hundred yards away, something moved toward us in the water. It moved so quickly the debris and water made a wake big enough to surf on.

"Levi!" I said.

He muttered something under his breath, and we shot through

the portal in the tree. He immediately closed it behind us. We laid on the floor of a corridor in the Otherworld. The musty smell turned my stomach. I rolled away from Levi and began to dry heave again.

"Grace," he said as he stood. My body still convulsed when he picked me up. The roots in the corridor reached out to touch me as we walked through. I'd seen them do the same thing to my father as the ruler of their realm, but I wasn't the ruler here. Each touch fed power into my body. I felt myself strengthening. Levi touched the roots as we went by looking for one close to home. "This one is out on the highway close to Dylan's house."

"Dylan's house burned down," I said.

"What?"

"Stephanie," I replied.

"I should have never left you," he said, kissing me on the cheek. "Let's use this one."

He reached out for the root. It curled around his hand as he opened the way. Voices floated down the corridor with the clanging of metal armor. "Hurry," I said.

"Stop!" one of the soldiers said as he rounded the corner. The emblem on his chest I did not recognize. A jagged knotwork crescent moon glowed as he approached us. We hesitated too long, and he rushed forward. Levi shoved me through the portal, but I clamped down on his wrist to pull him through with me. However, I felt them pulling him on the other side.

"*Let go, Grace,*" he said.

"*No! I won't let them take you!*"

"*They can't get you,*" he said, wrenching my fingers off of his wrist. Another cold hand touched mine and started to yank me back through. Putting my feet on the base of the tree as leverage, I pulled as hard as I could, but Levi was stronger. He had peeled my last finger off, then the other hand let go of me. I went flying away from the tree to the side of the highway just outside of Shady Grove.

"Levi!" I screamed, scrambling to get back to the tree.

"*I love you,*" he said, as the tree crumbled to dust. He had killed the root to keep me from coming back. Frantically, I started touching all the trees nearby, but none of them lead back to that same spot in the Otherworld. Running out of steam, the walk to town seemed too much to bear. I sank to the wet grass, releasing all the pent-up emotions.

My body shook with sobs to the point where I was gasping for air. I didn't notice when a car pulled over on the side of the road.

"Miss Bryant," Tennyson Schuyler's voice broke through my sorrow.

"Grace!" I heard Remy call out, then the slamming of a door.

"She's covered in blood," Schuyler said. "Miss Mistborne needs to look at her."

"Yes," Remy said, touching my cheek. He lifted me off the ground, but I didn't respond to either of them. Remy carefully lowered himself into the large car, guarding my head. The door shut behind us, then after a moment, Schuyler got back into the car.

"Back to Shady Grove," he ordered the driver.

"Yes, sir," the man responded.

"Grace, what happened?" Remy asked as he checked me for wounds. "We left after the wedding but made a stop at one of Schuyler's businesses before leaving town."

"Jeremiah's dead," I managed.

"Is this his blood?" he asked.

"Yes," I whispered.

"Where is Dylan?" he asked.

"Dead," I choked.

"No, that's not possible. He will rise, Grace," he said.

"I don't think he will this time," I said. I couldn't speak any longer except to say, "Brock took Levi."

"Bloody hell," Schuyler exclaimed. "This is bad. They are making their move now. Not on Summer. On Shady Grove."

"We don't know that yet," Remy replied. "It could be just a set of unfortunate events."

"Who killed Jeremiah, Miss Bryant?" Schuyler asked.

"Leave her alone. We will get answers later," Remy said, pulling me closer to him. "Call the doctor."

Schuyler dialed a number on his cell phone. The light from it illuminated his face. I could see the resemblance to my father now that I knew who he was.

"Miss Mistborne, please meet us at the clinic. Miss Bryant is injured," he said.

I heard her voice asking questions through the phone.

"Just meet us there. I am aware that the clinic is shut down, but I own it, therefore I have the keys," he replied. "Yes, yes. Bring them as well."

"Who else?" Remy asked when Schuyler hung up the phone.

"The wolf and his son," Schuyler replied rubbing his forehead.

The car pulled up in front of the now abandoned med center. The driver of the car took keys from Mr. Schuyler, opening the main doors. He rushed inside. Lights began to illuminate the rooms, as Remy carried me down the hallway to the emergency room. He laid me down on the first bed which didn't have any sheets on it. I heard Schuyler and the driver searching for items in the room. As Remy started checking my body for more wounds. He opened a drawer in a cart next to him, then rambled through it, pulling out a pair of scissors. He began cutting away the dress Dylan had given me. My heart ached.

"She is bleeding," Remy called out to them.

Schuyler walked up with a sheet in his hand, then looked down at me in horror. "Get that doctor here now," he growled.

"What is it?" I muttered. "Where is Winnie?"

"Just rest. It's okay. Tabitha is coming," he assured me as my eyes rolled back in my head, and darkness took me.

CHAPTER TWENTY-ONE

SUNLIGHT FILTERED THROUGH A WINDOW BESIDE THE BED THAT I laid in. I stared at it blankly. All the days of rain, and now the sun wanted to shine. I felt a cold hand slip into mine. Rolling over, I saw Nestor sitting beside me. Remy stood in the back of the room with his arm around Tabitha.

"Grace, how do you feel?" Nestor asked.

"Like death," I muttered. "Dylan?"

Nestor's eyes darkened, and he shook his head. "He didn't rise."

"How long have I been here?" I asked.

"Just overnight," he said. "What happened when the trailer went down?"

"Levi showed up. Our magic was blocked, but we used a tree to escape the sinkhole," I said. "But when we got to the Otherworld, the guards came up too quickly. He held them off while shoving me back here. Brock will kill him, too."

"No, he won't. Levi is too powerful. He will try to turn him first, but we know that Levi will never betray you," Nestor assured me. "We will get him back."

I was about to ask about Winnie, when Tennyson Schuyler walked in the door. "We have a problem," he said.

"What is it?" Nestor asked.

"Stephanie has called a town meeting. With no one to guard her, she's stirring up the masses," he said.

"I'll go down there," Nestor said.

"No, I will," I said, jerking the sheets off my body. "But I'm going to need some clothes."

"Out!" Tabitha ordered the men. They all left the room at her command.

"Thank you," I said.

"As your doctor, I'm ordering you to stay in bed," she said.

"You know that isn't going to work," I said.

"Grace, you need rest," she said.

"Is everything okay?" I said, holding my stomach.

"Yes, but you need to rest," she repeated.

"I'll rest after I kill a bitch," I said. "I should have done it before when I had the chance."

She knew better than to argue with me any further. Reaching into a duffle bag by the bed, she produced undergarments, a pair of cotton yoga pants, and a t-shirt. I held the t-shirt up to her and asked, "Where the hell did you get this?"

"I saw it in a store, and I knew you had to have it. I just haven't had time to give it to you," she said.

I slipped it over my head and despite the horror of the life I had to live now, I smiled at the shirt which said, "She's beauty. She's grace. She will punch you in the face."

"It's perfect," I said, marching out the door as Tabitha handed me a pair of slip-on flats. "Meet me there." I waved my hand and appeared outside the community center. The parking lot was jammed with cars. I could hear angry voices inside. Taking a page from Levi's book, I concealed myself after walking through the doors.

"Just calm down," Stephanie told the crowd as she stood on the platform at the front of the room. Devin stood behind her but only made eye-contact with his feet. "I know this has been a disturbing turn of events, but I assure you that I am just as equipped for the job as Grace was. Since we aren't sure where she is or if she is alive, I will humbly take her spot to lead this town."

"You were with Brock. We won't follow you," a man in the crowd shouted up at her. It was Lamar, one of the Yule Lads. Bless his peg-legged self.

"I am no longer with him. I admit my mistakes. When he tried to kill Devin, I had to leave him. My child was more important than anything," she said. "You need a queen, and I'm the only one here that can do it. No one else has the royal credibility."

"You are far from credible," Betty called out to her. "Get off that stage. You will never lead us."

"Maybe we should give her a chance," Mayor Jenkins said. "We need a royal leader."

At that point, the crowd descended into chaos. From my concealed position, it hit me that if I weren't leading these people, then my kingdom of Exiles would destroy itself allowing Brock to have free reign in the human realm. I still had supporters, but without Dylan or Levi, I wasn't sure my emotions could take leading these people. Part of me wanted to curl up and die, but I knew I couldn't do that anymore. My life was no longer my own. I hardened my heart, dismissing the pain. An icy chill flowed through my veins as I prepared to reveal myself. I walked steadily to the stage hoping no one could see me.

"Please. Be quiet!" Stephanie shouted, but the crowd didn't listen to her. She had no power here despite her weak attempt to seize it.

When I reached the top step, I dropped the concealment spell. Her eyes widened, and fear washed over her. She visibly trembled. Devin looked at me sensing my presence. I nodded to him to assure him that I wasn't here to hurt him.

"Silence," I whispered. The roar ceased immediately. All eyes turned on me. The back doors of the center opened, and Remy, Tennyson, Tabitha and Nestor filed in.

"You are no longer in charge here," Stephanie whimpered.

"The quiet of this room begs to differ," I said narrowing my eyes at her. "How dare you come into my town and try to take my place?

You are a sad excuse for a woman, much less a queen. I can't believe the deciding vote to keep you alive rested on me, and I allowed you to live. It was a mistake."

"You can't kill me. You voted," she said backing away from.

"I demand a re-vote per my rights as the leader of the fairy council of Shady Grove," I said. "Tabitha Mistborne."

"Death," she called from the back of the room.

"Nestor Gwinn."

"Death," he responded.

She began to beg. "Please my queen. I beg of you. Spare my life. I am a mother," she said looking at Devin.

"Is he really your son? I am doubting that among all your other lies. Betty Stallworth."

"Death," Betty said from the crowd.

"He is my son. He is Dylan's son. You would kill the woman who gave birth to Dylan's son!" she screeched in horror.

"He isn't Dylan's son," I said. "Amanda Maynard."

"Death," Amanda said, standing in the back of the room near Nestor. She held Mark's hand. I assumed the child was fine, but I didn't see Troy. And I didn't see Winnie.

"Should I vote to make it official?" I taunted her. It wasn't very queenlike but fuck that noise.

"He is Dylan's son!" she screamed.

"No, he isn't, because I am pregnant," I said. Her eyes flashed with panic, then abandoned hope. I held my hand up to snap my fingers when a portal opened up behind her. I couldn't see anything but hands, but they dragged her back through the portal. Her screams filled the room until the portal closed.

CHAPTER TWENTY-TWO

GRACE'S FACE DARKENED AS SHE KNEW AT THAT MOMENT SHE FULLY *intended to kill Stephanie Davis in front of her son. Devin was her son, but not Dylan's.*

"*Let's stop for now,*" *she said.*

"*You okay?*" *I asked, getting up from my laptop. She sank down into the couch and groaned.*

"*This part is just too emotional. I can't take any more right now,*" *she said. I sat next to her, and she leaned over on me. I pulled her closer and kissed her on the temple.*

"*Yes, but you made it through it,*" *I reminded her.*

"*It would have been easier if my bard hadn't been captured by my evil uncle,*" *she replied, taking a dig at me. She was fine if she was trying to upset me.*

"*When do I get to tell that part of the story?*" *I asked.*

"*I guess you should, but write it in your own story, separate from this one. The things you did to survive deserve their own place in all of this,*" *she said.*

"*My place in all of this has always been with you,*" *I said.*

"*Why must you be so damn sweet?*" *she asked.*

"*I'm not,*" *I protested. She turned to face me with a smile on her face.*

"*Yes, you are,*" *she said.*

"It's because I love you," I said.

"I love you, too, Levi," she replied.

I touched her cool cheek. She leaned into my touch.

"Is this when you read Dylan's story?" I asked.

She smiled, then laid her head on my chest. I ran my hands through the long platinum waves of her hair. Outside, I could hear the sound of a rumbling V8 engine. Winnie was home. After all this time, the Camaro still ran like a dream. Grace made sure of it.

"I remembered you telling me about the book. After I left the community center, I convinced Betty and Luther to take in Devin until I could find his real father. Their news about Winnie shocked me so badly that I retreated to the vault where Mike greeted me," she said. "You should probably be typing this."

"I'll remember. Just tell me," I said.

"Mike opened the door to the underground bunker without question. I ran down the steps to the vault, then stepped through the portal. I searched the shelves until I found the book you told me about. I pulled it off the shelf and ran my trembling hand over the cover. I had my memories back of the days prior to when Dylan and I were together, but I didn't know the whole story. I only remembered my side of it," she said.

"As it is for any memory, what you remember isn't the truth. It's just one side of the story. Sometimes you have to see both sides to find the truth. And only the truth can set you free," I said, sounding like a scholar. At least, I thought I did. She didn't.

"What utter nonsense," she laughed. "I love you for your nonsense though."

"Thanks," I muttered.

"Oh, don't brood. Or maybe you should. I find you irresistible when you brood," she said.

"This is me brooding," I smiled.

"Yeah, it looks it," she laughed. We could hear Winnie outside talking to someone. A male voice responded to her. "Mark?"

"Sounds like it," I said.

"Hmm. Maybe they made up," she said.

"It will be the third time this week," I said.

She laughed, then picked up her story. "When I opened the book to the title page, I laughed. Only you would think of such a ridiculous title."

"What? It was appropriate," I said. "Keep telling the story."

"*I waved my hand in front of the pedestal that was supposed to hold Taliesin's songbook, and a recliner appeared. It was the one from your apartment, by the way,*" she said.

"*I wondered what happened to that thing,*" I said.

"*It's in the vault,*" she replied. "*I sat down in the chair and read the story front to back in just a few hours. I teased you, but the title was perfect. Moonshine in a Mason Jar.*"

A MESSAGE FROM THE AUTHOR

As an independent author, I'm in charge of everything from writing the story to registering copyrights to marketing the book. One of the biggest marketing tools for an author is an honest review. If you truly enjoyed my stories, would you mind taking a few moments to review the books on Amazon? I would greatly appreciate it. Visibility increases with more reviews. As that happens, I'm able to produce more books.

Thank you so much for loving these stories. I'd love to hear from you anytime. Please message me on my Facebook page or through my email.

FACEBOOK: www.facebook.com/kimbraswainofficial
EMAIL: kimbraswain@gmail.com

REVIEWS ON AMAZON:

Bless Your Heart
Tinsel in a Tangle

Snake in the Grass
Comin' Up a Cloud
Gully Washer
Fairy Tales of a Trailer Park Queen Box Set

ACKNOWLEDGMENTS

I would like to thank the many independent authors who have influenced me or encouraged me. Not just in the Urban Fantasy genre, but from others as well. Indie authors have come up with some of the most amazing tools for a new author like me to thrive in this big business. I will be forever grateful for their help in realizing my dream.

My co-workers, friends, and family are always supplying me with the greatest stories about life that I can adapt into my books. It's amazing when one of them starts a story off with "you can use this one in a book." It thrills my author heart. Thank you.

My professional team are top-notch. I cannot recommend them enough. Hampton, my cover designer, makes me tear through the house just so I can see his latest file enlarged on my desktop. Carol, my editor, makes me cuss and love her at the same time. It is a magnificent feat. Erica, my formatter, gives great advice and is my go to for understanding the urge to buy a pre-made cover that I didn't really need. You guys are the best.

Last but not least, Jeff and Maleia. They are my Dylan and Winnie. My heart and soul. I love them so much and am continuously overwhelmed by their support for my dream. But when I think about it, they have always been the only dream I needed.

From early in life Kimbra Swain was indoctrinated in the ways of geekdom. Raised on Star Wars, Tolkien, Superheroes and Voltron, she found herself immersed in a world of imagination. She started writing in high school and completed her English degree from the University of Alabama in 2003.

Her writing is influenced by a gamut of favorite authors including Jane Austen, J.R.R. Tolkien, L.M. Montgomery, Timothy Zahn, Kathy Reichs, Patricia Cornwell, Kevin Hearne and Jim Butcher.

Born and raised in Alabama, Kimbra still lives there with her husband and 5-year-old daughter. When she isn't reading or writing, she plays PC games, makes jewelry and builds cars.

You can view my publishing schedule on my website:
https://www.kimbraswain.com/tentative-publishing-schedule

Follow Kimbra on Facebook, Twitter,
Instagram, Pinterest, and GoodReads.
www.kimbraswain.com

MOONSHINE IN A MASON JAR

FAIRY TALES OF A TRAILER PARK QUEEN
BOOK 6

CHAPTER 1

GRACE

THE GEAR SHIFT JABBED INTO MY SIDE EVERY TIME HE THRUST INTO me. This was my first chance to get laid in the last six months thanks to my contract with the Sanhedrin. I wasn't going to let a little discomfort stop me from getting mine.

I'd watched Joey Blankenship for a while before I ever approached him. He was young and worked hard, but he played hard too. He was twenty-five and worked for his father's lumber business. On the weekends, he went out with his friends, riding the powerlines. Mud riding was what they called it. I just knew there would be sex involved. I needed it badly. My frustrations were growing, but Jeremiah warned me not to give into my desires. When he called yesterday to give me the go-ahead, I cussed him for making me ask permission to fuck, then immediately stalked the town looking for Joey.

Joey was about 6-foot-tall with sandy blonde hair. He could have been Sheriff Riggs' brother, or perhaps a distant cousin. I didn't know what Riggs had between his legs, but when I found Joey at the Food Mart buying beer, I intended to find out what exactly he had.

I wasn't disappointed. However, his grunting increased and I knew he was close to a climax.

"Don't you dare come without me," I warned him.

He laughed as he thrust into me, "Then you better catch up."

"I mean it, Joey!" I said, trying to wiggle out from under him. He took it as I was playing with him. He wrestled me, laughing, but continued his business. I couldn't relax enough to get to that point. With one last shove, he groaned deep in his chest, and I felt it rattle around in his body. He throbbed inside of me. I was left wanting.

I shoved him off of me. "Get off me," I screamed. Scrambling from under him, I tried to cover my exposed skin.

"Grace, wait! Come on. I'll finish you," he offered.

I pushed open the driver's side door while pulling my skirt down. The panties I'd had on were ripped. He yelled behind me as my boots hit the mud around the truck where we had stopped to take a break. I turned to look back at him as he removed his used condom, then pulled up his pants.

"Leave me alone," I shouted at him. I trudged through the mud, but I wasn't fast enough. My boots mired up in the mud, and with my next step, the boot stayed stuck. I went barreling forward landing in the muck on my side. "Fucking hell!"

"Wait! Let me help you," Joey called out to me.

"I said, leave me alone!" I screamed. "You inconsiderate bastard! Don't you ever call me again!"

"Grace, I'm not done. We can go again," he said, rubbing his crotch to reawaken the beast. He had a good one. He just had no manners.

"I'm covered in mud!" I yelled back as he approached.

"So? It might be fun," he laughed.

"Fuck off!" I said, pushing myself up out of the mud. I removed my other boot, leaving it in the mud. Barefoot and covered in filth, I traipsed to the highway which led back into town. If I got lucky, maybe a farmer would let me ride in the back of his truck. Probably not though, considering it was already dark. Otherwise, it was a couple of miles, so I started to walk. I cursed Jeremiah, the

Sanhedrin, and Joey Blankenship. When I got to my trailer, I was going to pack my bags and go.

I hadn't gone a mile when I started cussing Dylan Riggs, too. In the distance, I could see his cruiser sitting on the side of the road with the interior lamp on. He could see me approaching, caked in mud. As if my night could get any better, there sat the man I hated the most on the face of the earth. The man I was forced to work with in town. The man who had chosen the other royal fairy.

This town and this arrangement had made a fool of me. My one chance to get laid, and the guy botched it. I suppose I could have stayed, but I was pissed. I hated this town. I hated its sheriff, but most of all, I hated myself for agreeing to stay.

Ignoring him, I walked down the road facing the town. Even when he called out my name, I didn't acknowledge him. I kept walking. When I heard him get out of his cruiser, I spun around.

"You go to hell, Dylan Riggs. Leave me the fuck alone," I shouted. He held his hands up in surrender.

∼

Download Gully Washer now!